D1534060

ALL YOUR CHILDREN, SCATTERED

Beata Umubyeyi Mairesse

ALL YOUR CHILDREN, SCATTERED

*Translated from the French
by Alison Anderson*

Europa
editions

Europa Editions
27 Union Square West, Suite 302
New York, NY 10003
www.europaeditions.com
info@europaeditions.com

Song "Ubalijoro" quote on page 118
© Rodrigue Karemera
Poem "La Môme néant" by Jean Tardieu on page 152
© Gallimard, 1951
Song "Akabyino ka nyogokuru" freely translated and quoted on page 181
© Cyprien Rugamba
All quotations translated by Alison Anderson

Library of Congress Cataloging in Publication Data is available
ISBN 978-1-60945-785-3

Umubyeyi Mairesse, Beata
All Your Children, Scattered

Art direction by Emanuele Ragnisco
instagram.com/emanueleragnisco

Original cover design: Création Studio J'ai lu d'après
© Shutterstock / Ivanchina Anna, MicroOne, Essl, VectorOK

Prepress by Grafica Punto Print – Rome

Printed in Canada

CONTENTS

For Mfurayanjye and Micomyiza

I reread the books I like and
I like the books I reread, each time with the
same pleasure (. . .): of closeness, complicity,
or better still, beyond that,
a long-lost kinship, found at last.
—GEORGES PEREC
W, or the Memory of Childhood

Umutemeli w'ishavu ni ijosi
The neck is the lid of sorrow
—*Rwandan proverb*

As she fell asleep, she placed one
soft hand over her land.
It was a gesture of belonging.
—BESSIE HEAD
A Question of Power

ALL YOUR CHILDREN, SCATTERED

BLANCHE

It's that time of day when peace ventures outside. Our killers are tired from their long day's *work*, they're heading home to wash their feet and get some rest. We let our hearts nod off for a moment and wait for dark night to fall so we can go out and scratch the earth for a yam root or some sweet potatoes to eat, a puddle of water to sip. Between them and us, the dogs, who have been running all day, begin to get drowsy, their bellies stuffed with a human feast their race is not about to forget. Soon they'll turn wild and even start biting into living, moving flesh, because they've figured out that there are no longer any borders between animals and their masters. But for the time being, tiny, clandestine peace knows that there's not a single living soul out on the roads that can capture it. And so, it can go out to greet the tall grasses as they straighten their spines on the hillsides, and the birds that stayed all day with their heads tucked under their wings, so as not to bear witness, so they'll never be called to testify at some tribunal, a day which will surely come; peace goes out to greet the flowers gorged with water from the rainy season, still struggling to exhale a fragrance of life in spite of it all, in a place where the stench of rot has seeped into everything."

That's what you would say when you still used to speak, Mama, your words full of holes, while you waited for your son Bosco to come back from the cabaret that night in 1997.

You would use the present tense, at that late hour of the

day, to share your memories of the month of April, 1994, as if those three years had not irremediably separated us. And the white wreaths of smoke that escaped from your hand, or came from my half-open mouth, yours *Impala*, mine *Intore*, two cigarette brands from *before*, the only ones we still wanted to smoke, as if to ward off the killing time—unless it was just a way to suffocate slowly on the effluvia of the past—our wreaths met and enfolded us in a reassuring cloud.

Sitting on the same wobbly little wooden bench as before, on the *barza*, the terrace, on the main road in Butare, and the broad trunks of the jacaranda trees hid us from the passers-by. You lapsed into your memories of the *month of milk that became the month of blood, ukwezi kwa mata kwahindutse ukw'amaraso*, between two moments of silence when you might just as well have been sobbing your heart out, and I listened to you, wondering whether my hand, which was itching to squeeze your wrist, might not startle you. So I did move, but blew my smoke toward yours so that it would reach you and loosen your clenched sorrow. Although I know nothing about chemistry, I recalled that lovely word, *sublimation*, from the time our teacher explained how solids turn to gas, and I thought there must be a procedure which, in the same way, would allow organisms that had become rigid to blow away in the form of smoke, without dying for all that, simply in order to meet harmoniously in the ether, invisible to anyone going by. I pictured myself as *Intore*, a warrior dancer with long ivory hair, carrying a blunt lance and a tiny shield of sculpted wood, whirling around you, *Impala*, hounded antelope, with your tortured horns, I'd surround you with a row of rescued words, resuscitated words. As the valiant *Intore*, with my arms outstretched, my back arched, I'd cause the earth to tremble, my feet would be decorated with little *amayugi* bells, and I'd cause the threatening enemy to retreat by vaunting your mighty deeds, your children, your lovers, your freedom that had come at such a cost. And while the night helped us to vanish quickly into the gloom of the *barza*, I listened to your voice, nodding my head, and if my movements were imperceptible, because I had long forgotten how to touch you, up there in the smoke I caused them to dance, those strands of white sisal decorating my brow like an *Intore*, dancing poet, ceremonial combatant capable of warding off your death, that month of April.

You fell silent for a moment, an incongruous pause in the middle of a sentence, you gave a start, let out a little cry, then a strange sound came from your throat. I thought you were crying, I looked closely at your face which stood out against the smoky air, the straight line of your nose was sharply lit by the last rays of the setting sun, I was afraid there was some brutal memory you might not be able to suppress anymore with your metaphorical language—which had protected me thus far, which had protected all those who didn't want to know how far the ignominy had actually gone, and all my courage as an *Intore* receded into my motionless breast. I waited, my stomach in knots, waited until I realized that you were laughing, quietly, with a jacaranda flower in your hands. It had fallen from the tree next to us, had frightened you, that childish fear which all through life threatens to resurface at twilight, despite ordeals valiantly overcome, despite reason procured by an *experience of the world.* You were laughing at your fear, no doubt also to banish the memories that had overwhelmed you in that brief moment when you had *told* me a little.

You lifted the flower to your nose and inhaled it for a long time, then you handed it to me, your gesture astonishingly delicate, in contrast to the abrupt movements and hieratic mood I'd found you in two weeks earlier.

With my index finger, I stroked the long little bell, its

purplish-blue color a perfect match for the twilight dying at that very moment over Butare. The wind had risen, rustling the dark foliage of the trees, and night fell all of a sudden, without warning, the way it does so well, back there. In the valley behind the bookstore, the frogs immediately began their croaking, in unison, as if they'd been waiting for a signal. I handed the flower back to you, you brushed it against your cheek then you tossed it on the dry earth at the foot of the jacaranda tree. I thought I could see your shoulders round despondently.

"Do you remember the story you used to tell us, Bosco and me, about the croaking frogs?"

You gave a little laugh which brought on the hoarse coughing fit of an inveterate smoker. Not far from where we sat, the sky, lit dimly by the moon, was riven by a flight of bats. Thousands of them lived in the branches of the pine trees in the arboretum, where the road from Butare leads away to the border with Burundi.

"Yes, I remember. So, what did they say, the frogs in your childhood?"

I adopted a storyteller's tone.

"'Tell me, frog, who goes there?'

"'Who goes there? The man who draws water.'

"'Has he drawn his water?'

"'Yes, his jug is full, I can see his heels disappearing down the path. Night has come.'

"'Well then, dear frogs, it is time to pray: Our father who art in heaven!'

"'Our father who art in heaven!'

"'Our father who art in heaven!'"

And as I was finishing my story, I laughed, too, with my voice still low like the pious amphibians.

We couldn't understand why the frogs repeated the first

line of the prayer all night long, and you told us that their brain was too small to learn the whole thing.

You said, "That was Bosco's favorite story," and without looking at you, I knew then that your distraught face was turning toward the lights of the cabaret at the far end of the main street; sometimes the sound of voices or snatches of Congolese rumba drifted to us where we sat.

You never stopped thinking about your son, even when, like that night, you granted me a fragment of closeness.

"Yes, I know it was his favorite story. He liked to pray, too, before he went away to war."

You didn't say anything, and in my mind, the echo of the words I had just said was so deafening that I closed my eyes and waited. Already I regretted it, I should have kept silent, or you should have answered so fast that we could have brushed my words under yours to hide them there. But you didn't say anything. For a long while. Two shadows passed, talking in hushed voices a few feet away from us, they didn't see us, or maybe they pretended not to. We could tell from the sound of their steps that they were wearing flip-flops.

"Both your fathers are in heaven now."

A dog, the one belonging to the *zamu*, the night watchman from the Hôtel Ibis across the street, barked just as you were saying that strange thing, and I wasn't sure I'd heard correctly. It was the first time you'd ever spoken of "our fathers." To regain my composure, I picked up a dry, oblong jacaranda fruit, and fiddled with it in silence. Were you at last about to tell me something else? Had the moment come to speak about *it*?

You groped for the pack of cigarettes on your lap, found it was empty, and asked me for an *Intore*. I waited, you lit it and smoked slowly, silently. My dry throat became a lid of sorrow.

I tried an indirect approach, speaking not about my own father, Antoine, but about my brother's.

"How did you know Bosco's father died?"

"Everyone knows everything in this country."

You amended your words, "You can find out everything, or suspect it. If one day you really love a man, and he ends up dying, you'll know the minute it happens."

Your confident manner exasperated me. What did you know about the love I might have for a man, Mama? What I thought I could read between the lines—that you hadn't loved my father as much as you'd loved my brother's father, and that's why you didn't know when he'd died—hurt me. It's so easy to draw definitive conclusions, to hide one's ignorance and act composed. Your words were as cutting as a revelation. I didn't know yet, at the time, that your confidence was a façade, so you wouldn't break down, and that the truth was locked away inside the words that weren't spoken, that might never be spoken. I reacted like a child, trying to hit back, with a nasty smirk.

"If everything can be known in this country, how can it be you didn't know anything about the extermination that was coming?"

You didn't answer. How can you answer a question like that? How could I have asked it? It was too late. An invisible, insidious border went up again between you and me.

I had just closed the breach.

Today, as I write these lines, I regret it bitterly. I know it was that night last year in Butare that with my heedless, choleric tongue I'd sealed off the only tiny opening you'd left me. It's too late to try and pick up the thread of our conversation, now that you've walled yourself up in the silence of a post-Bosco time.

You jumped up and declared, "I'm going to get your brother, he must be too drunk to find his way home."

You'd refused to let me go with you, "You know very well that things aren't easy between the two of you at the moment, go to bed, you need some rest before your trip home."

And you left.

My trip home.

I thought I'd made the trip home by coming to this house on the main street in Butare, where I'd grown up by your side. But for you, now, I was from "up there." Your son was the one who had come home, a revenant, and I was only passing through, an imported exotic plant that would have found life in your part of the world hard to bear, and which, in the end, had been repotted in its original soil. A Frenchwoman.

So I went to bed in my room. Could I still refer to it like that, that room I'd occupied for over twenty years? When I was standing outside the front door of our house, I'd gotten the queasy sensation that I was a stranger in my own home.

And yet nothing had changed in appearance: the building, which dated from the Belgian years, with a raised pediment that was a modest imitation of a certain type of Flemish architecture adapted for the tropics, was still standing, flanked by two majestic jacaranda trees in bloom, also vestiges of the colonial era. I'd found the row of period buildings intact, sober and run-down, on either side of the main street, which, as far back as I could remember, had been called the center of town. A July dust covered the *barza* where, sitting on *our little bench*, an adolescent was dozing, probably assigned to watch over the dozens of cases of empty Primus beer bottles piled up next to him. A recent sign in bright colors that hung above the door to the shop space that gave onto the street indicated that a general grocery store had replaced the fabric store that had been there before the genocide. Those rare times we'd spoken on the telephone, you hadn't given me any details about the new tenants of the place we'd always referred to as "the shop." You'd just said that Jeanne's husband—who'd set up his boutique selling *pagnes, kanga, kigoma*, poplins, Tergal and other textiles by the meter after the Greeks of Chez Christine's grocery left for Kigali in the late '80s—had done a lot of killing then fled abroad with his entire family. Along with the grocery, there was still the little restaurant, which you were now running with your sister. The same name, the same simple, welcoming décor. It was closed.

I stood for a moment leaning against the trunk of the jacaranda on the left, which was also covered in the laterite dust stirred up by the few cars that came down the street, and I studied the house, the paint on the walls that used to be turquoise and was now faded and peeling everywhere. I could feel inquisitive gazes on the back of my neck, coming from the terrace at the Hôtel Ibis and through the windows at the bank on the other side of the road. I didn't want to turn around, I hadn't seen a single familiar face the entire way from the bus station opposite the stadium, where the minibus had dropped off the passengers from the capital.

It was one o'clock in the afternoon, and Butare seemed anesthetized.

I listened out, hoping, in the hot air of the great dry season, to hear echoes of your voice or my brother's from beyond the gate that led into the forecourt of our building, voices to soften the thought of your life here, just the two of you without me.

I hadn't told you I was coming home.

What did I think about during those first hours back in my country?

I'd landed the night before, determined to spend no more than one night in Kigali, and to ask my new friend Laura to drive me the next day to the bus station so I could head south. She was the only person I had told about my trip, because I needed somewhere to stay in the country, and because I knew she would keep it secret for me as long as necessary; she was the stranger I'd met a few months earlier at my friends' from Bordeaux. When she had told me, in the course of a barely audible conversation, amid laughter and music, that she would be leaving the following week to work in Rwanda, I saw it as a sign. I decided that very day to buy a plane ticket, but I didn't know yet whether I'd have the resolve to use it. Laura was in her forties, and she wore both the taciturn expression of someone who has gone to rescue hope from the darkest recesses of the human soul and an astonishingly serene smile. The next day, I had coffee with her and I told her my whole story, all in one go, something I'd never done with anyone. Why her? I don't know. With my husband Samora I'd only shared snippets of my life, a few at a time, with extreme precaution, fearing no doubt that I'd make him flee or, worse still, make him feel sorry for me. Laura had convinced me that the reasons for my trip were well-founded. I felt ready.

Was I ready? On the flight from Brussels to Kampala, to Kigali, I spoke to no one. There were several UN agents, a Ugandan theater troupe that was on its way home from a little European tour, a few Rwandans, no familiar faces.

I listened, and kept silent, terrified.

When I left the airport, I breathed the air of the dark night, and all my tension seemed to evaporate. I hardly spoke to Laura on the road leading from Kanombe to the heights of Kigali where she lived with other humanitarians. I stared at the pockets of light the headlights of her jeep created in the darkness, on the lookout for some ghost. Trees, women, and men appeared then disappeared as if in slow motion; only the sound of the motor corresponded to the hurried beating of my heart.

The next day I awoke at dawn. I went and sat on the terrace of the house, wrapped in a blanket, to watch as the city below me roused itself, still caught in the mist rising from the valley. What had changed here? I couldn't have said, I hardly knew Kigali. But I recognized the sounds—the turtledoves singing "*sogokuru gugu! Nyogokuru gugu!*", the beating of the hummingbirds' wings as they flew, already, above the hedge of hibiscus roses surrounding my friend's garden. A smell of woodsmoke nearby, a motorcycle backfiring somewhere, then the voices of early risers carried on a breeze, people already on the road, greeting one another, "*Ese mwaramukanye amahoro?*"—"Did you wake in peace?"

So, people spoke casually of peace again, here, right from the break of day.

I took in every snatch of beauty offered to me that first early morning, fragrant with remembrance.

At lunch, Laura gave me what I wanted most—a plate of the fruits I had missed dearly: papaya, passion fruit, little bananas, plums, and Cape gooseberries. She knew I was anxious, and tried to calm me with a conversation full of complicity, telling me she'd come and get me at the end of the week to go to the lake, "You'll have had so much emotion to deal with, it'll do you good to go swimming at Kibuye."

In daylight, on my way to the bus station, I devoured the city, eyes wide open.

I took the first minibus headed for Butare. I insisted on sitting in front, on the worn leatherette seat, squeezed in between the driver and his assistant, who both looked at me with amused wariness. I had the look of a Westerner fresh off the boat, with my wrinkled trousers, tourist backpack, and it didn't tally with my fluency in Kinyarwanda, a complicated language which, to the best of their knowledge, no whites could speak without an accent, not even the old nuns who'd spent their entire careers in the hills. They did not show me the same polite reserve as the customs agent at the airport the day before. After he'd read my Rwandan name, *Uwicyeza*, detaching the syllables in a professorial tone of voice as if he were dictating it to someone, then my place of birth, he had said to me in Kinyarwanda, as he handed me my French passport, "Welcome, have a good trip home." This made me feel so emotional that I murmured, "Thank you very much," in my native language in a scarcely audible voice, but he responded with a faint smile. No one had ever greeted me like that, anywhere. There was nothing effusive about it, only the discreet assurance that I had come to the right place and had every right to be there.

I looked at the billboards recently put up to extol the country's beauties to tourists, and I pictured myself as this dancer with her brilliant smile and her arms raised to the sky, wearing a richly colored traditional toga, or that *Intore* dancer with his forehead circled by a sisal wig; I was even prepared to slip into the role of the huge gorilla in his setting of mountain greenery. I was from here, I had returned, and this stranger, a cousin wearing a kepi, born no doubt in exile in one of the neighboring countries where the Tutsis had fled to escape the pogroms between 1959 and 1973, had just confirmed it to me.

While the driver's assistant checked the other passengers' tickets and showed them where they must sit, which they did without complaining—it seemed my compatriots were still just as disciplined when it came to obeying orders—he peered at me out of the corner of his eye. The minibus left right on the dot, at the time indicated on the ticket, and I thought longingly of the bush taxis I'd taken during my vacation in West Africa the previous year, which would only set off once they had the requisite number of passengers, generally long after the time initially announced by the company touts; I recalled the cries of protest and the noisy farewells on the part of the voyagers, and the lively atmosphere that reigned in the crowded vehicle on every trip I took there.

My compatriots. I'd had to go elsewhere on the continent to realize how silent, secretive, and obedient we were, even austere in some respects. I belonged to that species: while the emotion of being back in my native country made me quiver all over inside—made me feel not only like throwing my arms around every strange woman whose face reminded me of my mother's or my aunts' or my childhood friends', but also like questioning every man I saw whose physique—wrongfully—made me think that he was Hutu, "What did you do, by the way, during the genocide?"—I remained mute and impassive and, in appearance, incredibly casual.

There were still empty seats in our minibus, and my neighbor on the right could perfectly well have gone to sit behind rather than stay beside me, but no doubt he was hoping, in this way, to glean some information about this strange crack-of-dawn female passenger. He was staring at the road, ears pricked, occasionally glancing at the half-open backpack I'd left at our feet. The carry-on luggage label of the airline I'd traveled with, Brussels Airlines, must have made him think I was Belgian. Did he not know that Air France had not flown here since 1994?

Once we'd left the Nyabugogo basin—which was beginning to get lively, requiring great vigilance on the part of the driver, not to run over the pedestrians who were walking carelessly and in great number along the paved road—he turned to me with his first question, simple but already too bold for our ancestral codes, where any sign of curiosity is held to be unseemly, "So, you're from here?"

"Of course, I'm from here, do you think I could have

learned our language this well anywhere else? I was born here
and I grew up here." I was surprised by the astonishingly serious tone I'd just adopted to say this, my voice resounding
inside me, in slow motion, as if I were hearing myself down a
telephone line during a storm. And I'd lowered my head, looking at my hands folded as demurely as possible in my lap. I
knew, because I'd expected it so often, the next, embarrassing,
question that would follow this injunction to reveal my origins—not my race as some people still put it, because you'd
have to be stupid not to notice my fair, slightly frizzy hair, or
the color of my skin, which was exactly midway between black
and white—in order to determine where to position me on the
border between Europe and Africa. No, it was the question
innocently asked of so many children, "Who are your parents?" So I waited for that question with the same anxiety as
before, and in my head, my rumpled thoughts were like a tired
white sheet from the long night of my absence, and in its folds,
I was hunting for a needle with which to resume my work of
memory. But wasn't that why I'd come back here, to stitch a
comma between yesterday and tomorrow, and pick up the
thread of my life? I waited. The taxi man didn't ask the question.

What had changed here?
Maybe the hundreds of thousands of former Tutsi exiles
who had come back after the war had imported other ways of
living, and people were no longer so concerned with working
through family trees—unless I've overdramatized the memory
of my interactions with erstwhile compatriots, those moments
of introduction where I felt as if I were dissolving, caught in
the trap of my skin color. I was surprised to see the conversation head in another direction, more sinuously. He didn't ask
me to talk about my mother, or about her husband. He said,
"Did you leave in '94?", and I nodded. Then he let an almost

complicit silence settle over us. He respected my reluctance to speak by stepping on the gas and, at the same time, turning up the volume on the radio, which was playing a Congolese rumba identical to the one that had been playing on Radio Rwanda three years earlier. I raised my head and let my gaze wander with the meandering of the blacktop road.

It was the high dry season, the hills were not as green as in the photographs in the *National Geographic* I'd found at a second-hand bookstore in Bordeaux upon my arrival, and which I'd kept tacked on the walls of the various rooms I'd lived in over recent years. The sky was very pale, almost milky, as if it had exhausted all the blue it had to offer humankind. Scattered along the roadside were mean houses with ocher walls, flanked with a single door left locked by the peasants who'd gone to their fields. A few passersby, children, with wooden hoops in their hands, their backs arched, their belly buttons protruding beneath clothing that was too big or too worn, cautiously watched the minibus go by, and when, just as we were driving right past them, they realized there was a white woman in the front seat, they gave a start, taken aback, too late to point her out to their friend, also barefoot, who was coming along the path behind them. Just time enough to hesitate between a frenetic greeting meant for me alone, or an outstretched finger to show me to the friend, at the same time as the word "muzungu" came from their rounded lips, and they let out a little cry that arrived distorted through the open window of the vehicle just before we passed them.

What had changed here? There were still children, lively and curious.

We went through Gitarama, Ruhango, Ruhashya, and Nyanza, where you went to secondary school, Mama. And when the minibus stopped in Rubona to drop off a few passengers, my heart lurched toward its confused memory of this place, where I knew you and my father had met.

When I was a child and we would drive past the big bamboo plantation that marked the turn for the Institute of Agronomic Sciences in Rubona, where you'd been working in the early '70s, your face would shut down abruptly and your voice would lose all inflection.

Lost in the distance of the hills, I held back the tears that were welling at the edge of my vision; those hills rolling by beyond the windshield, in appearance identical and unchanging, until I realized we had just been through Save. I hadn't had time to look, on the left, at the roof of the secondary school, adjoining what had been one of the first missions founded by whites in Rwanda at the beginning of the century.

I questioned the driver, stridently, "Was that Save?" and his laugh swept away the layer of awkward dust that had settled between us for a while already. "Oh! You really do know the country, don't you! Yes, that was Save, do you have family there?"

I liked his question. It meant that he'd fully accepted the fact I belonged here. No more conditions were set.

"My little brother was studying there, before going off to war."

He gave a start, making an abrupt gesture, and we very nearly struck a man who was laboriously pushing his bike, on which three huge bags of charcoal were tied, destined no doubt to be sold at the market in Butare. The driver's frown did not seek to hide the obvious question, posed only by his gaze, "And which army did he fight in?"

I didn't know anything about this man, his story, his involvements, no one was neutral back then, whatever you dared to hope. The past was too recent to be diminished, its deflagrations would still be haunting us for a long time to come. But I knew who had won the war, I knew that we had been *on the right side*, so I didn't hesitate to answer the question he hadn't asked:

"He enlisted with the *Inkotanyi* in '91. He was seventeen."

With infinite tact the driver murmured, "Did he return from the battlefield in peace, *Ese yavuye kurugamba amahoro?*" In this case, "in peace" meant "alive," and we exchanged our first smile when I replied, "Yes. He's in Butare, he's the one I'm going to see today."

I didn't mention you, Mama, in the conversation that continued quietly between the driver and myself, as we began the climb to Butare. I wasn't ready to talk about you to a stranger, you who survived here for a hundred days, you whom I'd abandoned at the beginning of April, '94: you were still a blind spot in the words I shared with strangers.

What had changed here? I had. The bitter, nostalgic gaze I cast on everything. What had been torn apart. I wasn't sure I'd have the strength to rebuild my relationship with you after three long years of silence interspersed with awkward telephone conversations and short cryptic letters.

Two hearts in tatters, meeting again.

Once I'd climbed down from the minibus, I walked slowly along the main road, my pack on my back, the curious gazes of passersby on my skin. I wanted to take pictures of everything—every wall, every intersection, the tall jacaranda trees aligned at regular intervals, the shadows they cast upon the pavement, the stadium, the town hall, the hedge outside Sarah's house covered with luxuriant bougainvillea, the post office and its shriveled old palm tree, the Hôtel Faucon, the former dairy, the partly uprooted street lamps, the faded sky streaked with clouds—everything made me reel with melancholy. My mind filled with conversations and faces I thought I'd forgotten; they began to spin and crash into each other like mad insects colliding inside my atrophied memory, as if it were the interior of a dried gourd.

I had arrived outside the house we'd always referred to as "home" with such a casual attitude that today I am struck by how false it was. The first "home" cannot be taken lightly, it belongs to the private sphere that remains buried deep inside us, no matter what happens.

I hadn't told either of you that I was coming.

I opened the gate and shouted "*Odi!*", in a trembling voice. In the gloom of the living room, on the other side of the little paved courtyard, Bosco's silhouette sat up and vaguely took shape, before appearing in the doorway. He did not reply with a "*Karibu!*"

I did not yet know that he had not come back in peace from the front, and that never again would he be in peace.

Immaculata

The day of your birth, Bosco, I wept every tear in my body. And it wasn't the pain welling in my mangled womb, or the immense solitude that overcame me that were the cause of my sorry state. No. The heavens were drumming ruthlessly on the maternity clinic's corrugated roof, the sound of torrents of water overflowing from the gutters drowned out the cries of the newborn babies, and their exhausted mothers were late in breastfeeding them. You were sleeping, impassive, indifferent to the displays of the high rainy season, or to the postpartum sadness that was delaying my milk. That attitude of apparent calm you've always shown, from the first hours of your life, and which you wore on your face like a mask—no doubt you'd already adopted it *inside me* when, back then, you'd had to cling tight to my uterus despite the jolts, despite the blows and the bars. You shall give birth in violence. You are softness, you give life. So many paradoxical injunctions that others arbitrarily tacked onto our lives, so many patched-up lies over thousands of years and which it is our duty to bear *with dignity* because one day someone decided that was the way things would be, and no other way. No doubt that is why we learn to tread a delicate path, very early on. To lie through our teeth, to accept, to slip comfortably into this accommodating fabrication. The maternal instinct: and so what. Because we give life more often than we take it, we owe it to ourselves to offer the human solution to the violence of men.

That afternoon the sky was roaring over our bowed heads, and I would have liked to leave you there and go and smoke a cigarette on the *barza* of the maternity ward in spite of the storm, in spite of my shaky legs. I would have given anything, too, for a cold beer, to ease my throat, parched from hours of crying and struggling. They'd had to open my belly with a scalpel to take you out. I'd heard the midwife say, "This one knows exactly what's going on outside, he'd rather stay where it's warm," before the anesthesia put me in a comatose state that I only emerged from a few hours later, with a dry mouth and a belly full of stitches. The maternal instinct—whoever invented it didn't know what they were saying, didn't have a clue, and wouldn't know what to do if it did actually concern them. Boastfulness and fraud. At our expense, that goes without saying.

Our hormones don't fill us with boundless love, no, it's time to put an end to that myth. If women kill less, often it's not because they're overflowing with tenderness, it's because they've had their fill of repressed violence, the one that inhabits the hollows of their fecund bodies, which belong to all of society.

The power of giving life, whether we like it or not: what a tragic farce. And what on earth am I supposed to do if I don't want that power, if in my guts I reject it?

I wanted to urinate but there was no one to help me get up, I wished I could have swapped you for a cold beer, and so I wept while I waited to learn to love you.

To give life. Together or alone? Always alone. To refuse to say it or share the news, or to say "our unborn child." That power, invisible. Men always stay on the threshold, in reality, they wipe their feet on the doormat, their gestures are clumsy, and they're immediately forgiven for it, because they're not supposed to *know how to go about it*, they stay or they go. If they stay, they become our heroes, if they go, we become *unwed mothers*. We know this, from the moment we begin to live together with this creature growing inside of us, and our fear of the man's decision becomes a constraint.

What happens after that, inside us, in the gloom of our breast, in our colonized body?

That's something no one has ever told us; we must resign ourselves to waiting for the verdict.

Do we have any choice? Did I have a choice? Did I make the wrong choices for you?

In a way, I did, in that way we could call fate, which was lurking in the prison in Karubanda at the dawn of your life. It's terrible, isn't it, my child?

I didn't have you on purpose.

I tried to chase you from inside me before it was too late, but no one would agree to help me. And so, you clung on. And I had you, violently, that goes without saying, because I knew, better than anyone, the nature of the grief the creature I was bringing into the world would have to bear.

So you arrived, with the stubborn air of those who know that nothing has gone as it should, and you were silent because it would have served no purpose to wail. I'd been weeping for months, and that day as well, my eyes put on the airs of an April sky in February. No, I didn't say to your father, "Our child which is in me," the last time I saw him. He was behind bars. You, too, when you were born, you were surrounded by bars. A wooden crib so that you wouldn't fall from up there. What no one knew, however, was that you had just started on a long and silent fall; the moment you were expelled from my body, you began to fall, with your vacant stare and pursed lips. Behind your apparent composure, which you would display your whole life long, my hands very quickly learned to detect the constant tension of a body waiting to strike the ground. People said, "This baby is too tonic, you have to massage him," and in the beginning I did as they said. Later they told me I had to get you to do sports, to help you relax. And on your days off, I made you run on the scorched grass of the Huye stadium. At the front, they must have thought your finger was too tense on the trigger, that you were too jumpy for some of the action. You'd simply been waiting for the impact from day one. And when you grew weary of waiting, you fired. For a brief moment, before death came again to immobilize your limbs, your body went all limp, a surrender that none of my massages, none of your running, none of your sleep—and you slept deeply—had ever managed to give you.

The only time I ever felt your back relax, your warm arms circling my hips like lazy snakes, was on the little twilit bench, the *barza* at the foot of the jacarandas. You would squeeze in between Blanche and me, holding a mango pit or a piece of sugarcane to chew on, and for a moment, you rested your ever-vigilant mind and succumbed to imagination, to join us inside the stories I unspooled for you every night like a thread. And in the dusk of the receding day, we wove the sinless lives of cicadas, the poem-prayers of the frogs in the valley, and the tales of *Bakame*, a clever hare that could outsmart the evil scheming of humankind.

Bosco. My accident-child. Your father probably never knew you existed, a son in free fall, when he might have proved your only safety net. He was transferred to a prison in the north among the *Bakiga,* who hated him; he left before you arrived.

I was set free. The prison doctor said to me, "In all likelihood he'll be premature, unless you lose him," and, incredulous, I thought, "He won't have a father, I can't start over, another fatherless child, I don't want to, I can't, I'm going to get rid of him." Then they let me go home after granting me a stolen instant to *say farewell to your lover*. They deliberately used the word *lover* because they knew it was a stain, would be a burden for me and his illegitimate offspring wherever we went. I was just a woman, not his wife, and I wouldn't have the right to visit him, once I went out the prison door. What can you say to your first love lying in a room with splattered walls, a man who's been beaten, who is distraught, what can you say about a story that unravels before it's even begun? "I have something inside me that belongs to you, too, but I have no intention of keeping it?" Big deal. I told him I'd wait for him; I knew it wasn't true.

I didn't mention you. We didn't have you on purpose.

Silence is a defensive weapon, cold and smooth, which a woman can use her whole life long against men, against her progeny, against herself. It's a prison without walls. Hang myself on my own tongue, isn't that what I did? Do you remember how we used to have a minister for the *female condition*? I always thought it was comical, just one woman appointed by the president to *be a voice for women*. Do they have any idea what that is, "a voice for women?" Those who say we are talkative know nothing about the rivers of words we never speak. What would happen if we *literally* began speaking, voicing our boundless desire for abortion, our exhausted desire for forbidden pleasure, our burning desire for absolute power? What would have happened if, instead of opening only my belly, the doctor had opened all of me, laid bare my heart, and my throat, so aptly referred to as *umutemeli w'ishavu*, the lid of sorrow?

Silence is my only shield. It wasn't upon your death that I stopped talking, my boy, I've been silent for far longer, and the tears I shed upon your birth, in my bed at the maternity ward, were all those words I knew I would never have to say again. I was getting rid of them once and for all, then, to make room for you, to become an *unwed mother* and accept the fact that from now on grief would be inherent in my status, that I must learn to live with the opprobrium other women now felt they had the right to heap upon me, that I would become an "incredible story" they could tell each other, reassuring one another that, unlike me, they had not dishonored the *female condition*—which, in those days, rhymed with decency and fidelity.

I did go on speaking, as if nothing had happened, out of politeness, to teach you to name the world: this is a heart, this is a flower, the cat is white, the hen is black, Mama is big, Bosco is little, Blanche is medium-sized, we're called family. Behind the carefully weighed choice of the inoffensive words I used for over twenty years, there was a viscous mass of all the things I had to keep silent, to protect you both from my blighted past.

Since I had to keep moving forward, I decided to do so with fewer words.

And yet, I really was a chatterbox once upon a time. Your father liked it. He would say, gently teasing, that sooner or later I'd get myself hired at Radio Rwanda. When we met, there were not many families who had a radio at home. People went *kuvumba radiyo*, to listen to the radio at a neighbor's who was equipped. Your paternal grandparents were among the privileged. That was probably one of the first things that Damascène, your father, told me. It was part of his charm campaign, because he already knew how crazy I was about music. He knew all the hit songs by heart, even the ones in English.

You remember?

My Bonnie lies over the ocean
My Bonnie lies over the sea

My Bonnie lies over the ocean
Oh, bring back my Bonnie to me . . .

I used to sing it to you on the bench at night, that one, and you and your sister would strike up the chorus, *"Bring back, bring back!"* He was the one who taught it to me.

Your father went over the ocean, you went to fight in the north, and whenever your absence, and his, overwhelmed me, threatened me with madness, I would sing that song, like a prayer, like a plea to fate.

You both came back alive, but everything had changed.

If only I'd known. How many women, and mothers, have dreamt of re-writing their senseless stories, in light of what they found out later, too late?

I will never blame God for what happened to me. In fact, I'm the one who chose the wrong prayer. Instead of asking him to bring you back to me, I should have begged him to let me go back in time. The art of unraveling one's life. Like what we used to do with those multi-colored blankets we knitted in secondary school with old balls of yarn the nuns were sent from Europe. You make a mistake, you start over. You learn new patterns, so then you undo the jersey, the monotony of knit a row, purl a row, so you can insert the stitches you missed. You see, if life could be like knitting, we'd know all we have to do is just remove the active stitches by pulling on a strand of yarn, tsss; just by pulling on the yarn. You go back, unravel your mistakes, and pick up the threads of your story.

I would have waited for Damascène instead of marrying Blanche's father. Or else, if that row in the knitting was already blocked, I would have protected myself better against your father's love and his destructive schemes, and I would have spared you a life of unhappiness. And no, once you were here, I never wanted to erase you, rest assured of that.

But you don't give a damn about any of all that now—my

remorse, my regrets, isn't that right, my son? Lord, what wretchedness! A crazy old woman who speaks to you all day long while you wait for eternity. A dazed woman pulling her hair out, clawing her breast, lamenting for hours on end with neither shame nor restraint. My poor child, I could have spared us both all that happened if I could have sent God the right prayers, efficient and targeted, instead of losing myself in an immature conjugation of the present conditional.

If only I could go back fifteen years, oh no, not even, I'm not that greedy, nine little years. Just before the war.

It's easy. I sell my house to a rich tradesman, request a passport, tell the authorities that you suffer from a very grave illness, in order not to arouse any suspicion, and I take us to live in Kenya—no, that's too close, you could still have joined the front from Nairobi, half an hour by plane wouldn't have been far enough away to steer you off course—France rather, or Belgium, no, to France, that way I could have taken the opportunity to arrange something for Blanche with her father. Yes, I'm sure that that way, everything would have come to a happier end. My God, but then, what about my sister, my father, my brothers, would I have had the right to save them from the coming catastrophe? And our neighbors, and friends, every Tutsi in the country, would I have been allowed to say to them, Run, run, you are going to be wiped off the surface of the planet?

How many people could I have saved with such a miracle, Almighty God, how many?

I listen out, but the only answer I get is the rain that has just started falling.

God knew what was coming and he didn't stop it. The foreign powers had been told of the existence of lists of weapons caches and of people to be killed. They did nothing to prevent our extermination. We heard the thinly veiled venom in the speeches on the radio, and yet for a long time, we clung to the hope that they would never act on their threats. Not with the whole world watching, not after all these years of progress. God and the world witnessed our elimination with their eyes firmly closed. Our cries, luckily for them, were stifled by the streaming downpours of the high rainy season.

I'm sitting in your little bedroom, on your bed covered in a silent dust of drought. The sky is clear beyond the window panes, where drops of water are trickling, clear beads that an invisible hand seems to have threaded evenly on a string of sisal. They follow each other obediently, sliding with delicate haste down the glass, pearling harmoniously, shot through with a ray of shining light before disappearing into the wall as it swallows hundreds of hurried opaline ghosts.

Time stretches on, indefinitely, a damp serpent pitilessly restraining me. I'm cold, I slip under the woolen bedspread I finished making just before the war broke out, to help you through the cold seasons.

That was nine years ago, an eternity.

I listen to the music of raindrops splashing on the corrugated roof. Is our Creator speaking to me in Morse code? All the sounds falling from the sky—the drumming rain, the sun making the metal creak, the dull plop of the fruit falling from the jacaranda tree—are they answers to my pleas? We can't go back.

If only I could have spoken to you—you asked me so many questions—when there was still time. Your sister, too, nagged me. Tell me his name, how did you meet, why did he leave? Where is he now?

Your fathers are in heaven now. And you, my Bosco, you're not by my side anymore either.

Not a single man here anymore. Because of me.

And now I'm crying, shedding useless, bitter tears over my fate. It's pointless to speak now. Do you see my eyes constantly going dark then lighting up, projecting the unbearable silences of the day before last into the air?

My sister tells the neighbors that I have gone mute with sorrow, and they all accept her random diagnosis. So many strange things have happened in this country, humanity went astray in such proportions that, for some people, just keeping on their feet, saying hello, still believing in the possibility of communication through an embrace is nothing short of a miracle.

People accepted my silence the way you accept another person's misplaced outbursts or irrational fear.

It's not my voice that has disappeared, listen: "Ah, oh, eeeh!" Sssh, that's our secret, and the others mustn't hear; it's my desire to converse that's gone.

When it's too late to speak, you keep quiet.

All these years, I have clung stubbornly to my belief that if I were to cleanse myself of guilt, I had to keep my story silent. I wasn't naïve, I knew that people hadn't forgotten, which became obvious to me when a stranger asked a subtle question about our atypical family. I let people gossip; I was moving on, into the present.

I couldn't stop them from talking to either of you. It was through them that you and Blanche, tired of waiting for me to give you answers, found out what had happened. What people told you was often an approximation, sometimes wrong, but how could I seem legitimate by acting offended, since I was the one who'd never given you the slightest shred of explanation? I said, "Don't believe everything you hear," but the snatches you picked up here and there—in the course of a conversation with my sister, or the maid, or a tactless teacher—had already begun to corrode the walls of your hearts.

As infants, you had babbled, unaware, and I could calm

your tears with a song, a kiss, or my melodious voice; the least little thing would placate you.

As children, you were curious about plants and animals, awake to the beauty of the days and the straightforward generosity of life—a piece of fruit, a laugh, and my stories in the evening under the flowering jacaranda, all filled you with a carefree bliss.

Then one day, without warning, I found myself face to face with the sharp gazes of dissatisfied adolescents demanding to know the truth.

Something between us had run its course.

And whenever I tried to begin to tell you, my sentences dissolved into unavoidable ellipses, lost in the memory of a trauma I could not bring myself to pass on to you.

I thought I was protecting you. I hanged myself on my tongue.

The tears dried on my cheeks, leaving a salty trace, a bitter taste.

Nine years to start all over again. I could still learn how to speak.

The rain has stopped, evening is coming, I'm going to prayer.

This song from church we loved so much keeps coming back to me, to my lips, sealed since you left—do you remember it?

Like a fragile breath
Your word is heard
Like a clay vase
Your love shapes us
Your word is a murmur
Like a secret of love
Your word hurts us
As it shows us the way.

Your word is a birth
Like release from prison

The rain has stopped, the heavens have fallen silent. God won't answer my prayers, even rewritten.

BLANCHE

They'd forecast snow for the day my son was born, but it didn't come. The sky stayed remarkably blue and sunny. He was born at the end of an endless night. The midwives said, "Your cervix isn't opening, your cervix is too narrow, it's no good," reprimanding me as if I were the one refusing to let him out. So they had to perform a cesarean at dawn, because he was beginning to struggle for air. The shrill cry he gave on coming out of me caused me to let go of all the tears I'd been holding back for so long, ever since I visited you in Butare eight months before that, Mama. And I don't know whether it was the joy I felt on seeing this proof of his existence, or the sorrow that you weren't there by my side, on that day of all days, that brought on that irrepressible flood of tears.

When his father took him in his arms, encased in his ridiculous green disposable hospital blouse, he couldn't help but start reciting a few lines that must have been constantly running through his head while his son was being extracted from my body: "Toward the very end of dawn . . . I could hear it rising from the far side of disaster, a river of turtledoves and savannah clover that I always carry deep within." It was like a profane blessing. Amused, the anesthetist asked him if he'd written it, and Samora replied ceremoniously, "No, sir, it's by Césaire," and the doctor—no doubt to show that he knew who Césaire was—found nothing better to say than, "Ah, so you're from Martinique, then!" It sounded like a summons.

I don't know whether Samora did what I'd often seen him

do when people would ask where we're from, namely, launch into an explanation about our respective origins, about the link between the turtledoves in the poem and the dove in his son's Rwandan name, or into one of his fiery speeches about Aimé Césaire, where he affirmed that the poet had forged his *Négritude*—his *Negro identity*, because as soon as they finished stitching up my belly, they transported me into a recovery room with white walls and a soft light where I instantly fell asleep, exhausted.

When I opened my eyes, he was sitting next to me, our baby in his arms. He kissed my hand, he must have been holding it for I don't know how long, then he handed me the little bundle without saying a word. When I put the infant to my breast, I felt a sensation I still find hard to describe even today: the impression that I was about to accomplish something I'd always known I had to accomplish, absolutely instinctive, natural gestures that must have been developing inside me for a very long time. With his tiny head against my breast, I was serene. I saw myself acting in a scene I'd watched a thousand times, painstakingly recorded in some remote place in my memory, with the sole aim of reproducing it myself, on that day.

But my son couldn't get my nipple in his tiny mouth.

The opening scene of motherhood I'd aspired to was being denied me.

I tried to force him, holding his parted lips with my index finger, while pushing the nipple in his mouth, but no sucking ensued, nothing. We were like two pieces of a puzzle that didn't fit, while an awkward child's hand tried to force them together. My persistence eventually made him cry and, distraught, I looked at his father; he took him from my arms again, and in his gaze, which sought to be reassuring, I could read a man's failure to understand when he is faced with an inadequate mother, a woman *who doesn't know how to go about it.*

Just then, I remembered another scene, buried in my memory for over fifteen years. The scene of a birth in the early misty morning in Butare. I must have been ten years old, maybe less. We were woken with a start by the sound of a man pounding at our gate, calling for help. You went to open to him, Mama, but only after quickly rolling a pagne around your nightgown—which was midnight blue with red polka dots, and I wonder as I write these lines how I can possibly remember a detail as precise as the color—after you quickly drank a few drops of water, instinctively obeying a cultural superstition, *kwica umwaku*, to destroy any bad luck that might befall a person if they speak to a stranger before they've had anything to eat or drink on waking up. I followed you out. Bosco, who hadn't heard a thing, was still sleeping. I tried to slip through the doorway, but you shoved me back inside; I withdrew, three steps behind you, but I didn't go all the way back inside the house, which was still full of the heavy smells of night. The man was holding a woman who was moaning, visibly exhausted and very pregnant. He explained that he'd come a long way, that his wife was about to give birth any minute, that he'd carried her on his bike from the hill of Zaza to go to the hospital in Butare, but the baby would be there before they could reach their destination. He had begged you, "Help us, please. God will return it to you."

I've never seen you out of your depth even in the most terrifying moments we've had to go through together. Maybe it's that strength that kept you alive in 1994, the strength to think on your feet, to make the decisions that saved you.

Now with this distraught couple you didn't hesitate for a moment, you said, "Come in," and you helped the stranger carry his wife into our living room. I noticed the bottom of her long dress was soaking wet. You laid her on the sofa and ordered me, in a low voice where I detected a restrained tension, to run and get Prisca, the neighbor who was a nurse and who lived nearby, behind the commercial bank.

When we came back, breathless, you'd already heated water on the little electric hot plate you only used occasionally, *to make it last*. In the meantime, the maid had arrived and was helping you fit clean sheets on your bed.

Bosco had been aroused by the sound of voices and pans banging and was standing next to the woman in labor, who was weeping silently. The husband, visibly overwhelmed, had gone out into the courtyard and was staring at the door, motionless, fiddling with his old peasant cap. And you, the impassive mistress of operations, you said to him, "Get back on your bike and go to the hospital. Tell them to send an ambulance. She'll have certainly given birth by the time you arrive, but at least she'll have proper transportation to the maternity ward." He had immediately obeyed, visibly relieved to have a *man's* mission to accomplish. Bosco was sent back to his room with the order not to come out without permission. As for me, no doubt because, even though I was a child, I was a girl, you let me follow you into your bedroom, where you'd taken the woman, and you let me stand and watch the birth from the threshold of the door, which I hadn't dared to cross, my eyes half-closed in fright. I remember that the woman didn't cry out, that it all went very quickly, the child was bundled in the new white tablecloth you had just bought from the Greeks, and when the ambulance came, long afterwards, you were smoking a cigarette out on the *barza,* talking with the neighbor while the newborn baby suckled its mother.

I couldn't breastfeed my baby.

And you weren't there, Mama, to take control, to work a little miracle, the way you had fifteen years earlier.

My baby had fallen asleep in Samora's arms, I motioned to him that I wanted to have him back, so I could feel him close to me, so I could ward off the estrangement I'd felt vaguely threatening us a moment earlier. I asked him to go for a midwife to help us.

I kept saying to myself, over and over, "If Mama were here, she would teach me."

One of my earliest childhood memories, vague and confused, was of you still breastfeeding Bosco. You'd nursed him until he was two years old, whereas for me, you stopped very early on, according to my aunt Maria. When I questioned you about your reasons, you assumed that frowning air you invariably took on when my questions forced you back onto the path of your accursed years, and said your milk had dried up because I didn't suckle enough, and that your sister, who fortunately had an infant the same age, had to feed me instead. I thought of calling you, it was winter here, an hour later in Rwanda, and I thought, "She'll be up already, she'll be happy to find out she's a grandmother. She'll tell me what to do." Then I thought better of it, I could already hear that mocking voice you sometimes had when it came to assigning blame for our dysfunctional relationship. You would say, "Like mother like son, he's refusing to nurse at his mother's breast, just like you did in your time." Maybe you would also point out that it was because I'd become too white here, that back in Rwanda you'd never heard of a woman who couldn't breastfeed her child, you'd send me back to my foreign body yet again, just like when I was growing up and you did everything you could to remind me of my difference. I was on edge, I didn't have the courage to deal with the slightest sarcasm, or any sudden violent outburst from your unpredictable way of being my mother. All I could do, to overcome this incomprehensible barrier that was looming between my son and me and preventing me from performing my inaugural role as a mother to the full, was place myself in the hands of a strange woman.

Samora came back, accompanied by a little black man with a shaved head, and gold-rimmed glasses on his flat nose. I sat straight up in bed, holding my sleeping child close; I was disconcerted. I'd heard through a compatriot that there was a man accused of genocide, a former gynecologist from the hospital in Butare, who was practicing in the region. So to avoid any untenable situations, before signing up with this maternity clinic, I'd carefully checked to make sure there were no Rwandan names on the list of practitioners. Could this be him? My panicked gaze went from Samora to the smiling man walking over to me. When he began to speak, to greet me, my fears vanished. He had a West Indian accent.

The midwife was a man.

He had a gentle manner and his warm fingers touched my arm with what I imagined to be the delicacy of an ideal mother. A natural understanding seemed to have arisen between him and my partner; no doubt they had exchanged a few words in the corridor on their way here. I knew my partner's mistrust of a man practicing a "woman's" profession could, to a large extent, be brushed aside through their sense of community recognition, something Samora valued above all else.

Here I was, having grown up in an exclusively female environment, and now I was discovering that a man could know more than we women did about the care required by a newborn baby. He patiently showed me the best positions for optimizing suckling, told me about the cream I should apply to my nipples to avoid cracks, described the signs and the way to control the flow of milk. Samora was looking out the window. Did he not feel concerned, or was he embarrassed by my nearness to the male midwife, this man who was touching his woman's breasts right there in front of him?

Despite all our efforts, our baby still didn't manage to suckle.

I agreed to hand the infant over to him so that he could examine it with his colleagues. I was once again overwhelmed with anxiety—a new and inward-looking variety. And I thought about you, Mama, the time you confessed, during the first days of the genocide, "I have almost nothing in reserve, I won't be able to feed you for more than a week, even if I completely go without." Now I knew what the responsibility of being a parent entailed. I thought, "Pray God this child will never know war."

The male midwife came back. He explained to us that the frenulum of our son's tongue was too short, that it was a perfectly common thing, particularly among boys. The next day, the doctor would perform a frenectomy, a removal of the frenulum which was easily done with a laser and which would "make it possible to free his tongue and restore its full range."

I learned how to pump my milk with a machine on wheels that made a horrible noise, I sent Samora to buy some fake silicone nipples and some nipple cream, and I complied with all the latest Western recommendations in order to "successfully breast-feed my baby." And my child eventually did begin to suckle.

I mourned the passing of my fantasy, that original image of motherhood.

The registrar of vital statistics came to my room the morning after the birth, but I had gone with my son to the operating theater for his frenectomy. So it was Samora who filled out the declaration.

I'd consulted you by phone, a few weeks earlier, about the choice of a middle name: I wanted it to be Rwandan. You suggested both *Kanuma*, little dove, saying, "It will be a symbol of the return of peace," as well as *Hategekimana*, which had been your father's name.

Samora, who thought it was a great idea to give him what he called a "native African name," immediately went for the first option. I was more doubtful. After Immaculata and Blanche, it seemed to me that a dove would be prolonging more than it ought to the reference to whiteness in our lineage. But the enthusiasm of the father-to-be, and the meaning of the grandfather's patronymic, "God alone decides," as well as the sound of it, too similar to the name of the former dictator *Habyarimana*, ruled out the second option from the start.

Was it the registrar who made the error, or Samora who didn't dare confess that he'd lost the paper where I'd carefully spelled out the choice of name in capital letters; had he been attempting to write a word in a language that was totally unknown to him, because he was convinced he'd remember it? "It's short, it's simple, easy to remember," he'd said, adding to the list of arguments in favor of *Kanuma*. Samora sometimes displayed the immoderate self-confidence of people who've questioned their own identity for too long.

The fact is that when we got back from the operating theater, after the first feed, still laborious but full of promise, Samora proudly handed me our family booklet where our son's birth had been recorded. Handwritten, in round, conventional letters, was his first name, Stokely, correctly spelled. I gave a start when I found that for the middle name a letter had been changed. Instead of the little dove *Kanuma*, I read—over and over, to make sure my eyes weren't fooling me—"Kunuma." Then I let out a nervous laugh.

"Is something wrong?" asked Samora, already busy rocking Stokely in his arms.

I showed him the wrong letter. The way he hesitated made me think he'd made the mistake.

"Kunuma. It means something else altogether."

His puzzled look. I'll never forget it.

"It's a verb in the infinitive that means: remain absolutely silent, become mute."

He apologized profusely, hurried, vague excuses, then he asserted, "We have to change it." I laughed again, almost amused by the idea, "Everyone in this family changes their name—you call yourself Samora, I swapped Blanche for Barbara . . . He'll just be following our strange customs, basically."

We had planned to call you that day to tell you about your grandson's birth. Samora had bought several phonecards to be sure we'd have time for a proper conversation, since calls to Rwanda were so expensive.

But I was tired, I didn't have the strength to go to the main corridor on the ground floor of the maternity clinic where the only phone booth for patients was located. I asked my husband to deal with it and, above all, to tell you that I'd call you the next day. You'd only spoken on the phone once since my return to France, when I told you at the same time that I was living with a man and was going to have his child. It wasn't particularly easy, either for you or for us. Your voice was full of worry.

"You're not married, my daughter, haven't you seen me suffer enough to be more careful? And this child, how will you raise it, you've only just finished your studies, and this young man I don't know, what makes you think he's going to stay, why should you trust a stranger more than you would your own mother? And where is Martinique, I hope he doesn't intend to take you there to live with him?"

The conversation had cost me a fortune, it had taken me over an hour to put your fears to rest. One by one, I'd answered all your questions with the calm manner of a nurse bandaging an open wound. Samora at my side couldn't understand a thing I was saying, he could see my tense face, could tell when I was arguing, he knew, because I'd told him, how easily words between you and me could turn awkward and hurtful.

I gave you all the details of our material situation, the way I might have to a social worker:

"Samora is already working, he has a good job as an accountant in a big company, and I've still got the job I landed at the end of my studies, as a nurse. Here in France, they give pregnant women a long maternity leave which allows us to go on getting a salary after the birth. I'll start work again when the baby is four months old. No, I don't have a maid at home to look after him, we got him a spot in a day care where very good people, professional caregivers, will look after him along with other babies. We have an apartment, and everything we need to look after the baby properly, we're going to get married very soon, before the birth. I won't be an *unwed mother*. Samora's mother is as French as they come, and she'll help us raise our son, and as for his father, well, he didn't know him, he doesn't know anything about him except that he was from Martinique, it's a French island in the Caribbean, you can look on the map, he's only been there once so, no, we have no intention of going to live there. Everything will be fine, Mama."

A few weeks later, I sent you a photo of our quick trip to city hall, promising that we'd come and celebrate our wedding with you in Butare as soon we could, and I got the impression that now things were headed in the right direction. You wrote me a long letter where you gave me a thousand and one tips about how I should lead my life now, as a wife, so that my relationship would be solid and last to the end of our days. I kept it preciously in a shoebox with all the mail I've kept from the years when we still used to write, these envelopes that came from Rwanda but more often than not had been mailed from France or Belgium by people passing through Butare with whom you'd entrusted them. When the Rwandan postal services finally began to work more or less efficiently, I was filled with nostalgia on seeing those stamps from before with their naïve drawings. How many years did it take the new state to print its own stamps? Everything had to be redone—the national anthem, the flag, the banknotes—to turn the page and build a different national identity. I suppose stamps were not a priority. Nobody wrote to each other anymore, they phoned, and before long they'd be sending emails. The stamp on your *letter of advice to a young bride* represented an *iboza riparia* plant, that very bitter medicinal plant that Rwandans swear can cure anything, the *umuravumba*. I wondered if you'd chosen it deliberately, a way of warning me against the heartache that was lurking, of telling me that bitterness is an integral part of a successful marriage, by which you meant a marriage that lasts until the end of the final day, and that I would have to subjugate the astringent memory left on my lips by the end of the first day's kisses. Rereading your letter today, I can imagine the treasure of imagination you had to come up with to tell me about the life in a relationship you hadn't known, a life you hadn't known; in all likelihood you were repeating things your own mother had told you on the day of your union with my father, that oh so lovely marriage that had lasted only two years; you were professing principles that were the exact opposite of what you had experienced. Your history must not be repeated, I had to run from the lights of passion that had lured you away, destroying your respectability, depriving your children of a home that would have been reassuring, because it would have been conventional.

I was so hoping that the birth of this grandson would bring you solace for the difficulties of raising two children on your own, amid public opprobrium, and would restore the smile the genocide stole from you.

One child, the birth of a dove, *on the far side of the catastrophe.*

IMMACULATA

Anastasia, my mother, had a reedy little voice. She was one of those women who always seem to be apologizing when they do speak up, or who have only delicate secrets to share. She made her way through language with infinite precautions, giving the impression that she weighed each word before she said it, that she knew its precise weight and, consequently, could foresee the impact it would have on the ear, and on the heart, of the man or woman who heard it. Words can be sharp, can pierce brutally like a spear, crush like the studded truncheons the killers used to smash our skulls in the spring of 1994. Words are often like pretty decorated calabashes, hollow and cracked underneath their shiny surface, or treacherous—when a snake has hidden inside, using the night to slip along its narrow neck and fill a heart with suspicion or enmity. And my mother, who mastered perfectly the double entendre of our language, was careful to use such words sparingly, not to hurt anyone, not to suggest the slightest echo of hostility after a conversation that had seemed innocuous in appearance. "Nothing we say is innocuous," she sometimes said, "nothing can be left to chance. That's how misunderstandings arise and foster resentment, which in turn provide a bed for hatred, where slaughter can germinate." She never failed to add her favorite proverb at that point, *ineza irenza umunsi, inabi ikagaruk'umuntu*, "The good you do will enable you to survive, the evil you inflict will come back to you." As she said it, she was probably thinking about how our Hutu neighbor had helped us during the killings in 1959. To thank him for his protection, her husband had given him a cow; she wouldn't live long enough to see the sons of that same neighbor wipe out her family in a bloodbath, never mind witness the way he forgot to repay the kindness she'd tried so hard to show them her whole life long.

Bosco, my boy, your grandmother was an excellent embroiderer. She had learned the art late in life, when my older sister Maria came home with thread and cloth from the Family School, the establishment for girls who couldn't attend the high school and who had no other horizon than to become meticulous, *enlightened* wives, by learning to sew, embroider, cook, and keep a *modern* household of the kind you'd expect in those years just after independence.

Maria was bored to tears and furious she hadn't been admitted to the secondary school, because she wasn't a bad student. But since only a small minority of Tutsi, and only the most brilliant, had been able to land a place in the science section, she was chomping at the bit while waiting for a husband to liberate her from her crochet and her weaving.

Anastasia found a treasure of imagination with the colored threads and the needle my sister always left for her at the end of a brief *family* exercise. She sewed the way she spoke, with a fine hand and parsimony, never making a mistake. Most of the time, her conversation was the reflection of her embroidery patterns: full of abstraction. Her cross stitch created overlapping triangles, and her proverbs never said either yes or no but rather, "Think about it twice." Do you remember the doilies that used to decorate our living room? She made them all!

You were still just a child when she died, Bosco, and I don't think you saw her very often with one of her projects in her hands, quick and focused, absorbed. And yet that's the image that springs to my mind when I close my eyes today. She loved you both so much, you and Blanche, I even think you were her favorite grandchildren, probably because she thought you were the most fragile. She always stood up for you when a fight broke out with your cousins, or your grandfather reprimanded you too harshly.

She was a whisper-woman, and her hands were always cool like spring water, even when she was working in the fields under the sun. She would listen without flinching to her husband as he fussed and scolded her all day long, and she remained impassive when others would have answered back or raised their voice. She would probably have liked for her two daughters to develop the same temperate nature, and she warned us, "When you have your own homes, avoid yawning without reason; your husband is another woman's son, what you say will never be worth much to his ears; avoid peddling juicy gossip, honey is just as delicious when it sticks to the fingers of those who steal it, so the bees can find the thief, and will come back and sting; just as surely, malicious gossip inevitably comes back to slap the face of a woman who has delighted in it and spat it back out like a succulent stalk of sugarcane."

When she was silent, sewing or going about her other activities, Anastasia hummed a single melody that we were never able to connect to a known song. The same tune, over and over, as if to fill the space and ward off any temptation to come out with words she might regret. Like the smell of the eucalyptus leaves she crushed and slid into the hem of her pagne every morning, this nagging little tune that followed her everywhere wove a strange atmosphere around her which, as we grew older, began to weigh us down and seemed suspicious to others. One time I came upon a neighbor who was telling her she must be a little crazy; another time I saw two of her cousins exchange a meaningful grimace behind her back. Our mother's melody of silence hung over us like a constant cacophony, like the crackling of a radio that cannot pick up a single shortwave station.

Was it in reaction to my mother's silence, and my sister's constant sullen moods, that I grew up as noisy and talkative as they were discreet and quiet? Maybe it was just my personality—the way yours, Bosco, was to be taciturn. They told me I bawled continuously from the day of my birth to the *kwita izina* and *kurya ubunnyano* ceremony, which was held eight days after I came into the world.

My brother Théophile, ten years older than me, loved telling the story in great detail—until his death, he was the finest specialist in the traditional rites of our household. Eight children from the family—four boys and four girls—were invited. They were given little hoes to go and weed the earth behind my parents' house, then, when they came back, they were made to wash their hands and feet before they were settled on a mat in the courtyard, with a big woven tray in the center covered with banana leaves, where their meal had been set out: red beans, taro, amaranth, and above all, little balls of cassava paste symbolizing a newborn baby's droppings. All accompanied by fresh milk or junket. According to Théophile, I screamed throughout the entire meal, so much so that my mother, who was not supposed to get up as long as I hadn't dirtied my diapers, broke the taboo, preferring to run the risk of a curse if it meant she could shut us away inside. Once they'd eaten the vegetables and drunk the milk, each child went up to my mother and me to give me a name that would symbolize the course of my future, or the qualities they wished for me to have. Everyone suggested variations that suggested the need for serenity or silence: *Utuje* (the calm one), *Uziguceceka* (the one that knows how to be quiet), *Nyirakiragi* (the silent one).

It is said that at the very moment my brother Théophile said

"*Nyirakiragi*," I fell silent. And that is why my father decided to give me that name. Immaculata would arrive a few weeks later with my Christian baptism, in honor of an old aunt who had died recently.

No *kwita izina* ceremony was held for you. When you were born, Bosco, I had not yet gotten my house back, I was living with Maria and her husband, the three of us in a little room we rarely left; I was trying to make us forget those wicked tongues that were working to spread the story of my fall from grace. My father very nearly disowned me for dishonoring the family. I had no more friends, no more husband, no one to invite to your party except my mother and my sister. We gave you a name and had you baptized in secret, as if we were burying a cumbersome corpse. I called you *Muhoza*, he who consoles, without great conviction; it was practically a girl's name, which just goes to show.

For Blanche, there had been a major ceremony, on the same day as my wedding with her father Antoine, and her religious baptism. It was my mother who chose your sister's Rwandan name, *Uwicyeza*, a name which has two meanings, as I would later realize. But at the time we just translated it for my husband as "It means that she's the most beautiful." Four of the eight children present were the offspring of his expatriate French friends, as well as the son of my Belgian boss from the Institute of Agronomic Sciences. For their little Western stomachs, we replaced the taro with potatoes and the cassava with meatballs. They still went ahead and ate with their fingers—a source of great amusement to the Rwandans present—then they drank some Coke instead of junket. The Rwandan mothers forced their children to drink the fresh milk, which still smelled of cow, the poor children kept glancing over in the direction of the red cases of fizzy drinks, trying to honor their tradition while dreaming all the while of being little white children. I was the one who chose the name *Blanche*, which made Antoine laugh, "She's only half white, you think by calling her that it'll make her a little whiter?" But he gave in, acknowledging that it was a pretty name, and he couldn't see why he should deprive his daughter of it just because her skin was brown. As for you, I called you Bosco simply because I wanted both of my children to have names beginning with the same consonant. If her name had been Marthe, we would have called you Marc or Melchior.

My parents were beaming with happiness that day, proud to see that I had finally *made it*. Our civil wedding had been held in a panic a few months earlier, when I was already very pregnant, and without any regard for the tradition of asking for my hand or the dowry. This angered my father and my brother Théophile, who celebrated practically all the rites on the hill and were proud of being the last guarantors of the region's ancestral traditions.

The grandeur of our religious wedding was meant to make everyone forget those failings. I had a long gown that was bought in Kigali, with a little tulle veil hanging from a plastic headband, which made me look, spuriously, as if I were taking my first communion, and Antoine agreed for the first time in his life to set aside his sandals and khaki shorts in order to wear polished shoes that matched his suit, sewn by the best tailor in the Arab quarter and made with the most expensive cloth from the Trafipro cooperative in Butare, still flourishing in those days. My father gave a long, fine speech. Then he drank a bit too much Primus and spent the rest of the evening dozing in his armchair, an enigmatic smile frozen on his lips. Was he thinking about the first time he ever saw a white man on the hill, as a child, how it gave him such a fright that he hid behind a bush until he could hurry down the hill "faster than a goat being chased by a famished hyena," as he used to tell it during the long evenings of our childhood spent in Ikomoko? In his address to the guests, he said that, beyond the color of our skin, God had created us identical, capable of procreating to give the world beautiful mixed-race children, who in our time were reconciling the sons of the colonialists and the daughters of the colonized. As I translated for my young husband, I was careful to tone down this historical reminder with its political undertones, as well as the innumerable references to the Bible scattered throughout his text: my parents had no idea that Antoine was an atheist and had only agreed to be wed by a priest after a night of tears and threats on my part. My father didn't mention love: it must have seemed inappropriate to him on such a day.

As usual, I spoke a lot and loudly, above all in French to our Western guests, to show my former classmates how far I'd advanced socially. In my young mind, the future could be nothing but an uninterrupted flow of bliss.

My sister Maria saw to the logistics of the meal with the efficiency of the seasoned tradeswoman she was, and the inhabitants of Butare and Ikomoko said that, in living memory, they had never eaten so much meat nor drunk such quantities of beer.

I would boast of it shamelessly for weeks afterwards, mindless of how that schoolgirl childishness could come back and hit me right in the face, much later on, too late, when the wind turned. Too much of a windbag and you'll eventually blow away. I should have learned to keep quiet earlier on in my childhood, instead of constantly chattering.

At primary school, my teachers wore themselves out trying to get me to keep my mouth shut, with the help of switches from eucalyptus or lemon trees. Windbag, the daughter of Hategekimana and Anastasia, was constantly being punished. But in spite of the scoldings and thrashings that left long welts on my arms, I continued to cackle like a hen that's pecked at hot pepper.

I learned to read very young—the magnetic pull of words, to give them shape in my mouth before I let them go, a rosary of letters to mumble, an endless prayer for my lips that were never closed. I learned everything that was written on the slate by heart, and on my way home, the long road I walked with my sister, I recited "a e i o u" at the top of my lungs; she walked faster and faster to try and leave me behind, while what I left behind was stories and secrets, along the path at the foot of the tulip trees and the scrawny mango trees; the playground at recess was full of those stories and secrets, and I was the appointed chronicler.

You had a lovely reedy voice, Bosco, I haven't forgotten that, no I haven't. You got it from me, that's for sure. Sometimes I found you humming in the house when you thought you were alone. Beneath your mask of indifference there was a boy who was moved by the slightest melody; you always pricked up your ears when there was music on the radio in the living room. If I'd encouraged you to learn to play an instrument, to sing in a group, maybe you wouldn't have gone to war?

At the secondary school in Nyanza, I joined the choir with genuine joy. While I had never been tempted to gaze at my own face in a mirror, and I almost instinctively avoided looking at the reflection of my tall skinny body in the windows of the dormitory, I fell in love with the tessitura of my voice. From our singing teacher, a Canadian woman whose accent was terribly exotic, I learned that I was an alto, and those four letters became a source of thinly veiled pride. In the shower, or during my cleaning chores at boarding school, I would proclaim "alto" out loud the way I would have said "bravo." The girls who became my best friends, my confidantes, Léocadie and Jeanne, gently made fun of me, "Oh, you're all set to join the angels in heaven, don't sing too loud or else the Lord will want to hire you for his choir up there!" We rehearsed the songs for Sunday mass two evenings a week, and I put so much passion into it that in no time I knew by heart the words to all the anthems, offertories, and other hymns to Mary.

In the beginning, I hardly understood what I was saying, because we'd gone from classes that were solely in Kinyarwanda—with the exception of French class—to being absolutely forbidden, once we were in secondary school, from speaking our mother tongue.

Any girl caught exchanging a few words on the sly in what the white sisters called the "native dialect" was handed a ridiculous white cotton cap and a slate on which was written, in white chalk, "I'm a dunce." She had to put up with the jeers of her classmates in silence, when they were quick to "heehaw" like donkeys in her face.[1] And she would keep an eye out for the first classmate who made the same mistake, to hand the slate on to her. Informing became the only means of ridding oneself of shame. None of the pupils had ever seen a donkey, other than in the drawings the head sister had shown them upon their arrival, nor had they ever heard any braying other than that which came out of her big mouth along with her rare, horsey smile. The white sisters had not tried to find out whether there was a word in the children's native tongue to describe weak or disobedient children, which they could have simply translated into French. We read texts that described wheat growing in the fields of faraway Wallonia; we learned to perform plays in which strange musketeers fought to recover the diamonds belonging to the queen of the kingdom of

[1] In French-speaking countries, the conical dunce's cap also has a pair of donkey's ears, and is known as a "donkey's cap" (*bonnet d'âne*). (T.N.)

France, we learned poems by heart that heralded the coming of spring after a long winter, on the banks of a little stream which, as we were duly informed, had its source near the Mont-Royal cemetery. On paper, we learned about seasons, mountains, the Himalayas, and also Kilimanjaro—closer to us, but it seemed just as improbable as all the rest to young girls who had never even seen the volcanoes in the north of their own country, less than a hundred and twenty miles from Nyanza.

As for me, I was never caught speaking Kinyarwanda. The first weeks, during recess, I would shout at the top of my lungs the only two words in my repertory that seemed appropriate for the situation, "*A moi! La balle!*"[2] Until silence fell. We were souls to be saved, dunces living on borrowed time.

I remember one evening, a few years before the beginning of the war, I sang you songs I'd learned phonetically those first months of secondary school. You and Blanche had such a laugh! Our little bench creaked to the rhythm of your hands clapping whenever you managed to recognize a word of "real French" amid the gibberish.

The choir was my first refuge. When I was singing, even if I had only a vague idea about what I was saying, I totally grasped the meaning of the melody, and I was in absolute harmony with this little woman who had come from far away and whose thin arms bobbed up and down abruptly to show us the way. I never got lost when there was music, but surely would have without it. When I missed my mother, I would hum her little gently crazy tune; when I missed my hillside in Ikomoko, I would let the shepherds' lament rise up inside me: my brother Théophile had taught it to me when we used to walk home from school in the rain.

[2] The ball! Over here! (T.N.)

It was in Nyanza that I encountered modern music, the kind that was cut on records or that came out of the radio. Pure magic. My first love, long before your father. It was Sisters Magdalena and Léontine, the youngest ones, who gathered us in the refectory on holidays and played music from their countries for us. We were allowed to dance: they taught us how to waltz, and later, I would teach you, in our living room in Butare—you would goof around, whereas your sister remained very focused; they also taught us a few ballet steps.

On holidays our choir sang mass together with choirs from other secondary schools in the region; exceptionally, they allowed boys and girls to mingle.

We paid special attention to our hair on those days, and the blouses and skirts of our uniforms were ironed with more zeal than usual. We knew we were going to be scrutinized. Particularly those of us who stood on stage to sing. The first few years, I was too young—and probably also too much of a "peasant," as the town girls put it, grimacing disdainfully—to understand what was really going on, the closely watched language of seduction: the dance of eyelashes, motionless burning gazes, discreet brushing of shoulders. I kept my eyes riveted on the whirling hands of the sister who was beating time, then I hurried to sit back down and stare at my feet, before returning to the dormitory with the other youngest pupils, without dawdling on the way.

My mother, who watched me leave after vacation with a body that was getting visibly curvier, began to inundate me with warnings: I was too young to be thinking about boys. I believed her, I promised her, I tried to cultivate a discreet manner that only my voice contradicted. My only love was music. The time for boys hadn't come yet. I listened distractedly to the older girls' overexcited whispering, as they spoke about this boy or that boy who'd slipped her a note, an ardent letter, as they were leaving church or stepping down from the bus. Sometimes I wondered, however, if I'd have the right to any of that someday, too. In the meantime, I danced and sang and my body grew, beginning to turn like a ripe plant toward an unknown light that my mother dreaded.

Now I understood all the words of the songs in French; love didn't have a face yet, only hundreds of refrains to express the first quiver.

And then I met your father, Bosco.

I forget what we were singing that day, it was for All Saints, we'd decorated the altar with lilies and white carnations, it had stopped raining but it was cold, I was wearing a cardigan the same color as the faded sky. My forehead burned for a long time from a gaze I could sense riveted on me before I dared to find out where it was coming from. Your father was sitting in the second row. That very night, I entered into the dance of whisperings in the dormitory, of gazes interlocking when we passed each other in the days to come, of wandering thoughts on the slope of desire.

Then there was a first note, signed "Damascène," a song copied out in fine, careful handwriting; I haven't forgotten the couplets. A song I sometimes used to dance to with you when you were a baby in my arms, without telling you how much it upset me.

Decades later, all it took was for one of those songs from my years in Nyanza to resound, and time, and the years that had crushed my early enthusiasm, would be erased, and once again I would let myself be carried away by the same wave of uncontrollable emotion. To hear a melody from your youth, from those days when possibility carried us beyond the hills, with an urge to dance, hands raised with the grace of my eighteenth year: rheumatism disappears, bitterness dissolves, I'm that fragile young woman in the gaze of her lover-to-be, and all the tension of pleasure that hovers on the horizon is held in the curve of my back, the tilt of my neck, which he touched yesterday with his trembling hand, in my moist lips sustaining the tremolo, and for a moment I have my whole life ahead of me.

You left too soon, my son, to know the nostalgic epiphany that a simple tune can give a tearful old heart.

When Stokely began primary school, his parents signed him up for a workshop in an introductory music course.

They'd always had record albums at home. Samora's: Otis Redding, John Coltrane, Richard Bona, Miles Davis, Son House, Bonga, IAM, Nèg' Marrons, all of Gil Scott-Heron, and a few biguine classics. Black men.

Blanche's albums, women: Miriam Makeba, Barbara, Nina Simone, Khadja Nin, Jeanne Moreau, Billie Holiday, Anne Sylvestre, Cesaria Evora, Cécile Kayirebwa, and cassettes of Rwandan music from the '80s and '90s.

Two pairs of ears, two sensibilities. What did it depend on?

Each of them listened to his or her music when the other one was absent; it seemed that Congolese rumba from the '90s—and not always—a few hits from OK Jazz, Cuban *son* and Scott-Heron were the only tastes they shared, even though on the surface their tastes seemed quite similar.

Samora and Blanche loved to dance. Before Stokely was born, they would go to all the parties their Afro-Caribbean friends—students, the unemployed, or young workers—organized in dorms or little apartments in the Saint-Michel quartier, filled with laughter and rhythm. Even after an exhausting day, even the night before an exam, they could find the desire to go and sway to the music, and in everyone's opinion they were the most handsome couple, the best dressed, and they could not be beat on any improvised dance floor.

As if to force their respective mothers to lie—both of whom had refused to acknowledge that either child possessed the famous "sense of rhythm" that was supposed to inhabit anyone with black or mixed-race skin—together they learned to master the steps of the salsa, the rumba, the zouk, and the soukous, which they performed with casual mastery for their hosts, who could only admire this eminently well-matched couple.

In the early weeks of their relationship, they had established their own particular ritual. Whenever they went out, they would first spend a long time choosing matching clothing; she would complement her hairstyle of the moment (braids, afro, or smooth hair) with artificial flowers the same color as their outfits, and he began to wear hats (going to the flea market for his Panamas, flat canvas caps, Stetsons, berets, and Borsalinos). Then she would leave the house first, flamboyant. Twenty minutes after she arrived, he would make his entrance, a dandy of the African "*Sape*" variety, and after he'd given out a few fist bumps to his mates, and kissed Blanche's girlfriends effusively, he would pretend to see her for the first time, to be subjugated by her well-rounded hips, to discover how well attuned their styles were, and he would go over to her ceremoniously and say, "Madame, would you be so kind as to grant me this dance?" The party could begin.

Then she fell pregnant.

Those first months, she went on dancing as if nothing had happened. When her tummy was plain to see, in all its beauty, she swapped her colorful outfits for a long black dress that was comfortable and elegant and that clung harmoniously to her mother-to-be figure. The flowers she always wore on her head echoed the hues of the father-to-be's tie or shirt. They were resplendent, closer than ever, they arrived together now, and only got up for the slow dances; they drank fruit juice and went home early, accompanied by the more indulgent but still admiring gazes of their circle. Her girlfriends said, "He'll be a perfect father, he stopped smoking and drinking when you did, he's so responsible." And she thought, confident: "Yes, I found the right one, we'll be a model family." They owed it to themselves to succeed where their mothers had failed. She still believed that the fractured framework in which they had grown up was due solely to inconsequential women who hadn't known how to keep the fathers in the nest.

They had moved into a bigger apartment on the rue du Port, to be ready for their son, Stokely—Samora had already chosen his first name as an obvious tribute to the Black Panthers' honorary prime minister. She had painted the walls of the nursery yellow, "to tell him the story of all the sunshine in the world"; Samora'd had one of his women friends from Senegal sew curtains and an entire range of bibs, sleepers, and diaper bags made of pagne. Above the cradle, Blanche hung a mobile fashioned with banana leaves that she'd bought at the craft cooperative in Butare during her trip in 1997, when she did not yet know she was pregnant.

And for the first time, they listened to their respective records together. Their favorite was the Afro-Cuban All Stars he'd given her on their first Christmas, exactly nine months before the birth of their son.

Where other parents might worry over how much religious education they should give the fruit of their loins, and to which God they should dedicate him, Blanche and Samora thought only of controlling the sounds that entered their child's ears. Where others would be teaching their child to walk, they already wanted to see Stokely dancing, to prove that he, like his parents, had a *sense of rhythm*. They gave him tambourine cuddly toys, maraca rattles, and harmonica-fish for the bath.

Under this regime, Stokely quickly acquired a good ear for music. Very young, he began to beat time on the coffee table with wooden spoons; he would start to wiggle the minute a note of music could be heard. His parents were delighted, and while they'd stopped going to their friends' smoke-infested parties, they never missed open-air concerts in the park, or festivals where they could hear African and West Indian groups, jazz, or salsa, at times that were compatible with the baby's sleep. They even started going to the traditional Bastille Day ball, where they gently mocked "those Whites who don't know how to dance" and their disjointed hopping around to soulless, corny pop music.

They would gaze at the *Conservatoire de musique*, a large, imposing building a stone's throw away from the rue du Port, with all the wariness and circumspection of the poor in the presence of the cultural institutions of the elite. It was therefore with a certain trepidation that they agreed for their son to take part in the "first steps in music" program, the fruit of a partnership between their boy's school and that institution, and offered to all the children in kindergarten without discrimination.

Neither one of them had ever had the opportunity to learn to play an instrument or been taught to read music. It was an unknown world, which they looked upon with the rather hostile respect of the illiterate for a dictionary. They had never thought of music as something that can be learned sitting down, that can be written on a piece of paper, or that can exclude instead of bringing together.

When her son came home and began to tell her, his voice vibrant with emotion, about the bassoon, the French horn, the violin, the flute, and the oboe, Blanche told herself that her worries had only just begun.

"And the bass drum, Maman, oh, it was so huge, the bass drum!" he said, over and over, all evening long.

"We know how to write French flawlessly, how to speak without an accent, we've read a ton of books, many more than most native French of our condition; we've had some higher education and we can prepare recipes *du terroir*. But that music, that language—we know nothing about it, it has never spoken to our souls, it is a cold and distant continent that leaves us stiff; how can I go there with my little boy, without utterly failing?" Blanche wondered.

They went together to the multimedia library to borrow the records the conservatoire had recommended.

Vivaldi, Tchaikovsky, Chopin, and Saint-Saëns came into their home. Little Stokely didn't dance anymore, he listened and hummed, keeping the tempo with one finger raised, to imitate the orchestra conductor he must have had a chance to admire during a concert for children with their teacher. One evening, while listening for the fourth time to *Peter and the Wolf*, his parents could not help but indulge a reluctant fit of laughter, and they had to face facts: "Stokely likes white people's music."

Raising our own children makes us view our own parents' erratic work with greater understanding. Struggling with her ignorance when her son asked her questions, Blanche recalled how angry Immaculata used to get whenever she'd asked her for help with her math or English homework in Butare. "You ought to pay closer attention in class, little numbskull! I've been keeping you clothed and fed all this time. You think I have the leisure to take evening classes or go to university while you sit there yawning with boredom instead of writing everything down and asking questions to people who know?" In her anger there was all the resentment she'd never voiced against a system that would not allow a young Tutsi girl, however brilliant, to attend university, all the shame absorbed when she used to listen to her French husband talking with his ex-pat friends, and she'd recognize the words but was unable to grasp the humor or the innuendo, all the resentment against her condition, fueled by thousands of tiny humiliations accumulated since childhood—because she was a girl, because she was poor, because she was a Tutsi.

She had done her best, just as, no doubt, Blanche wanted to do her best now, to go as far as she could with her son into a world she'd never had access to. It had taken only three generations for the transmission of the keys to life, which up to now, had justified the authority of the elders over their descendants, to become obsolete. Immaculata had left the hillside, and the skills in cultivation and husbandry she had learned from her parents, who in turn had learned them from theirs, and so on, all the way back, were no longer of any use to her. To Blanche, from the vantage point first of her French school, then of university, her mother's secondary school education seemed ridiculous. Every time, the field of what was possible had grown wider, deeper, casting the older generations to one side, while earlier and earlier the child called into question the significance of the labor of those who had come before, their culture, their values.

To guard against a breach that risked widening between her and her son, Blanche decided to learn his new language, to share his passion. Too many walls of silence had gone up already between the members of her family. When Stokely began playing the clarinet in first grade, she signed up for an adult class and began learning at the same time.

On weekends they began talking about tessitura, reeds, Mozart, and Brahms. Samora felt left out and adopted the role of the complainer, saying over and over that he didn't like the sound of that language, where one white was equal to two blacks, and he went so far as to question the origin of the ebony wood with which their clarinets were made. Their son paid no attention; his mother, her mind always on the alert to ward off the slightest rift, suggested a compromise, "When we get good enough, we'll be able to play your favorite jazz standards."

He replied, in bad faith, "Trumpet, saxophone, piano—those are the instruments Black jazzmen play. The clarinet is a white man's thing. Besides, you can't dance to it."

"That's not true, there have been Black clarinetists right from the beginning, they're just not as well known, and anyway, stop always looking at things through a lens of melanin!"

Their first clashes:

"You cater to his every whim, don't let him start thinking he'll be able to join some major classical orchestra, they'll always remind him he's not the real deal, he'd do better to devote his time to his studies."

"He's in grade school, it's important for him to have something to be passionate about. When I was that age, no one believed in my dreams."

"And what were your dreams? Go to Europe and find your white father who never gave a damn about you? Sometimes it's better to warn children what the outside world is really like, that way you spare them a heap of disappointment."

"Don't you go ruining my son's childhood with your resentment. Times have changed, Stokely is French, this is a new generation, more mixed-race, more open, less rigid."

"And I was born French, too! And that didn't protect me, young people are racist nowadays, too, stop being so naïve! Even if he becomes the best clarinetist in France, even if he becomes famous, the journalists will always introduce him as 'a second-generation immigrant.' Always. They'll try to turn him into an Uncle Tom, a collaborator, their token Negro, like Satchmo."

"Not a chance, with the name you gave him, they're more likely to stick a threatening feline on the posters next to his name."

"Or else they'll tell him to change his name, or change his life."

And for the umpteenth time he would tell her the story about the great South African singer Miriam Makeba who, at the height of her fame, saw all her scheduled concerts canceled in the United States because she had married Stokely Carmichael, one of the leaders of the Black Panther Party.

More often than not he would calm down, but there were times when they would pointedly turn their backs on each other and fall asleep without another word.

But there were still a thousand and one moments of shared joy, in the morning when they woke up, when they put on *their record* and all three of them danced with their arms around each other to the sound of the piano, trumpet, maracas, and suave, elderly Cuban voices, before it was time to go out to confront what the father called *the hard realities of the world*.

After Blanche had been learning the clarinet for three years, Samora found himself unemployed, in the wake of a redundancy plan several major private companies implemented, while new buzzwords in the newspapers—*pensions schemes, stock options, golden parachutes*—masked a faceless crisis, and Blanche had to stop her classes and put in additional hours at the hospital. In the tram, after a long day, she would listen to the pieces her son was learning to play, and she'd let herself be lulled by the rhythms that still sounded strange to her ears, while she was inhabited by a beauty she finally admitted could be universal. Father and mother no longer went dancing, even on Bastille Day. They watched with pride as their son became more confident, his fingers fluttering along the black ebony and the white nickel silver with an elegant dexterity that reminded them of the mambo steps they used to dance. At the end-of-year concerts at the conservatoire, they would look around for other *dark-skinned* people, whom they acknowledged with a complicity the other spectators would not have understood: "We are not the only ones who dare," was what their exchange of smiles said. When Stokely turned ten, they took him to the Opéra, to see the first Black conductor the venerable Bordeaux institution had ever had—a Canadian originally from the same island as Stokely Carmichael, Trinidad—directing a sonata by Bach for oboe, clarinet, and bassoon, and a Gershwin concerto. They had dressed in matching colors, she wore flowers in her Afro, he had a new hat on his head. Stokely, who didn't feel concerned by these matters of skin, simply informed his parents that they were *way cool*.

BLANCHE

How do you charm a man, Mama? Which gestures, which gazes, to let him know you're attracted to him, without covering yourself in shame or looking like a whore? A *malaya*. That was the word you used when you wanted to scare me. If you don't behave properly around men, you'll end up like the *malayas* in Tumba, up there on the hill past the university, those women who sleep with anyone solely for the money. It was a recurrent warning, a dark horizon which your grave tone, your brows frowning with inquisitive concern, made me imagine with deep fear, but also a hint of curiosity.

One day, on a visit to your friend Mama Doudou, who lived not far from the row of little houses along the street you had twice pointed out to me as the place of perdition, I went out into the street to play with the other children, fueled by my desire to see *all that* closer up. I must have been around fifteen at the time, and as the oldest in the group, I was in charge of looking after the others. It was a Sunday afternoon, I suppose it was right in the middle of the rainy season, because I remember the red mud clinging to our sandals, the ball that splattered our legs when it hit a puddle, a low gray sky. I sat down on a damp tree stump, sideways to the street, so that out of my right eye I could spy on what was going on across the way, in the *malayas'* house, while pretending to be interested in the ballet of children having fun. A little adobe house, long and narrow, four rooms stuck together one after the other, and each had its own door with tiny windows on either side of it. The doors, with their wooden frames, were all made of the same cheap corrugated iron that was used for the roofing, and they stood open, while cloth curtains made it impossible to see inside; I imagined it must be small and dark. Two young women, dressed as was usual for a Sunday afternoon to do odd jobs around the house—old pagne tied around their hips, loose faded T-shirt, hair hidden by a casually knotted scarf—were sitting outside the house on little wooden stools. A child who was roughly a year old was resting between them, seated on a mat on the ground, trying at regular intervals to stand up by pressing against one of the women's buttocks, his mother's no doubt, while she was leaning over a basin wedged between her feet, energetically scrubbing clothes in water that was white with foam. The other woman was smoking and snapping the ends off beans. They seemed joyful, and exchanged loud greetings with the few people passing by.

I imagined that at any moment a "client" (I'm using the word today, but I doubt I knew at the time that the men were referred to like that) would stop in front of one of them, and that after a lengthy negotiation she would get to her feet. It would surely be just like any transaction at the market, wouldn't it? She would boast about her assets, her youth, her beauty, while he tried to get her to lower the price, it was the end of the month, he hadn't been paid yet, he would point out the competition, her neighbor seemed every bit as appetizing, etc. Then she would wipe her hands on her pagne and eventually lead him into the room, pulling the door closed behind them.

I figured that after that they *would do it* in silence. I wondered when he would pay her, before or after? And then, would they come back out together or separately? Could you read the effect of *what they had just consummated* on their faces, the way very spicy dishes made your brow sweat, or beer made your eyes shine? And the baby? If the woman he'd chosen was its mother, would it start crying when it saw her go away and shut herself inside with a stranger? Would the other woman take it on her back to calm it down and stop it from disturbing its mother while she *worked*?

Nothing of the sort happened. The only man who stopped by them was an itinerant cigarette salesman to whom the woman smoking had called out in order to buy a box of matches and some chewing gum. I was disappointed. My little scheme must have been obvious to the two women, because after a while, one of them waved to me, inviting me to come over, "*Yewe,* you, come over here, I have something to tell you!" I turned my face, not trying to ignore them, and I stood up and crossed the street, which just then was deserted. They were smiling at me. The one who had called me over wiped her dripping right hand on her thigh and held it out. I shook it, silently. "You're Immaculata's daughter, aren't you?" I nodded, intimidated. "I know your mom, we were in elementary school together." This information, that there might have been closeness between them, even if it was long ago, seemed incongruous. As I went on standing there, motionless, visibly ill at ease, the woman said, no doubt to release me from the awkward situation, "It's about to rain, take the little children home and give your mother my regards." I mumbled something and went back across the street without turning around. She'd been right, raindrops were beginning to fall and it was easy for me to convince the little group of Mama Doudou's children to go back to the house. When you saw me, you asked me why the back of my skirt was wet. I think I must've had a very guilty expression on my face as I explained that I'd been sitting on a damp tree stump, to keep an eye on the others.

On our way home we went past the *malayas'* house again, but the women had vanished, and I didn't dare pass on your former schoolmate's greetings.

I was fifteen years old and I couldn't imagine that any dealings with the body of a man could be the source of anything other than shame or opprobrium.

Seduction is a tricky thing. Far away from you, I learned to tremble like a petal in the wind, I discovered that particular lightness of touch, and gestures that speak of the undertow of a heart set free, touch that melts and terrifies. I found my way all by myself, Mama, in spite of your fears, counter to the absurdity of your warnings, your lessons about prevarication in the presence of pleasure (a horizon that, above all, must not be reached), and about the abject traps hidden behind words of love.

With Samora, far away from you, fortunately.

It happened with a simplicity I would never have suspected, given all your wild imaginings. It was the third time I'd seen him; we had danced all night long a few days earlier at a mutual friend's, he had something more than mere charm, his hair was light and frizzy like mine, his gaze disarming. Above all, he had that obvious self-confidence I had always lacked. He was waiting for me, unexpectedly, outside the entrance to my nursing school.

It was raining, the way it often rains here, a blessed weather for those who want to get closer. I had a big rainbow-colored umbrella, he offered to hold it over our heads, I held his elbow with my hand, it became a household altar, a firm warm receptacle for the boney hardness of his warm flesh, my hand seemed meant to hold that arm, the way a foam mattress curls around a languid body on the verge of sleep. It was enough for that nesting to last all through our journey for the skin of his elbow and the palm of my hand to say to each other, "Here, yes, now." Our enchanted lips said nothing, they waited, our steps like a moment of suspension led us to the dark entrance to my university residence where I invited him to "wait for the rain to stop." I pressed the light switch, and in the cold artificial light of the huge foyer, our lips waited one last moment, then a muffled clap of thunder from outside signaled the moment when at last they could meet, wordlessly, in the same élan as our yearning bodies, as our clasping, rain-wet hands. The dripping umbrella at our feet was the only witness to this first embedding.

For a long time Samora had wanted to be whiter than white. No one believed in it, except for him. In the little village in the Médoc where he grew up, there had been no lack of *nicknames* repeatedly relegating him to his status as a Negro. But he chose to live in denial. It was only once he became an adult that he changed color, or at least accepted the color he'd always been. He said he'd had an epiphany when he came to the city, to Bordeaux, where for the first time he had access to texts by Césaire and Fanon. "I'm the one who has chosen my condition, yes, no one else imposed it on me," he still likes to say. I let him talk, if it can help him to see things that way . . .

In reality, he cannot truly be either, and that's his whole tragedy. He is one of those people who believes that life is drawn solely with lines and straight angles, who ignores all the latitude given by curves, hidden bulges, bubbles that go off on a tangent, who pretends not to see the terrible monotony of parallel lines. As if mixed-race people could only ever choose between white and black, as if a child could only ever be either its mother or its father. Even gone, even absent, or maybe above all, when he has simply vanished into thin air, a father's color clings to our skin. His absence marks our brow, flays us within, creating a tortured flow of mixed blood in our body. It is everyone else, those who believe they have the luxury of being a single color, of being indivisible, of blending into the reassuring mass of their fellows: they are the ones who tell us we must choose, who categorize us, crucify us.

You too, you often crucified me, Mama. Like every time you said, "You can't do that, don't forget you're white," "You don't know how to dance, sit down; your stomach isn't solid enough for *urgwagwa*, drink a Fanta instead; if you do your braids like that, people will see how light your scalp is; if you come to this market with me, you'll drive the prices up." But there were times when you forgot to remind me of my difference, when you let me be just your child, just a girl who had to be taught to hide her thighs, or her budding breasts, to walk taking measured little steps like any other *well-brought-up* Rwandan girl. I liked it when you said, "you" to mean my cousin Francine and me, we were undifferentiated, practically twins, born the same year, and we got our period the same year. We became prey to men at the same time, a source of anxiety to our mothers on the same day. Francine is surely the only person who never reminded me that I was different: was it because her mother had breast-fed us and weaned us at the same time? Later, my aunt would tell us how she used to hold the two of us, one on her left, the other on her right, how we would keep our eyes riveted on each other while we were greedily suckling the milk it seemed would never run out, "When you weren't hanging from my bosom, you shared everything that your baby teeth, which came late, could chew: bananas, sweet potatoes, slices of avocado. You never argued over the pieces, and you learned in no time how to show a united front whenever Thierry and Tharcisse, my two eldest, mounted an attack and tried to steal your share, which was often."

Sometimes it's in your gut that stories get woven, and your brain isn't even aware of it, Mama. Francine and I drank the same milk at exactly the same time. The day she was killed, I threw up continuously from morning to night, I couldn't keep anything down. I had just arrived in France, so at the time I thought it was the change of diet that was to blame, but when, later, I heard how the militia opened her belly, the one that had digested the same milk I had, I understood.

You see, people have been coming here from elsewhere forever. Italians, Russians, Portuguese, Moroccans, Malians. The language of their fathers and mothers was passed on for one or two generations, but there were times when it was lost sooner because the children had to become real French citizens. Their names, which are transmitted officially from father to child, cannot be erased completely, even when they're truncated, as with some Armenian names, where they remove the suffix "-ian," the names remain and spread through society more or less indifferently, more or less tensely. Sometimes the trace is lost through marriage, brides easing into French names with either the relief that they'll no longer hear their last name mispronounced, or the regret of giving up a little by erasing a lot.

But what stays longest, Mama, and this I realized very quickly, is the memory in your belly. By perpetuating the flavors transported in the suitcases of exile, by passing recipes on from mother to son or daughter, the descendants of a shared distant ancestor buried in Algiers, Kraków, Dakar, or Barcelona create a community of taste that never yields to the eradication of one's origins.

Even when nostalgia has dried up, and the old yellowed photographs no longer interest the younger generations, there are still dishes that render in today's language the fragrance of childhood, of feasts and laughter in accents hiding deep wounds, separations, silences, that cannot say their name. All the ancestral curses and antiquated fairy tales, which one spice will suffice to revive.

When I first got here, I immediately sought out the places where I might find "a taste of home," but nothing was the same; neither the West Indian sugared plantains nor the foufou from Cameroon could come close to the *ibitoki by'inyamunyo* bananas you used to make, with freshly crushed peanuts and white eggplant, or the *ubugali* with dried *sangalas* when it was the end of the month and you had to make ends meet. I've learned how to cook French, with French produce, and as my belly has grown, it has forgotten you all, a little.

As for Samora, he had never known any cuisine besides his mother's, her family from the Médoc that went back ten generations; only a short-lived relationship with a young Martinican who'd come to Bordeaux to study law had derailed her temporarily from a life firmly rooted in this part of the world. It was the son who had decided that his father must be a lawyer; in reality, his mother had never told him anything more than, "He was a student, it was the end of the year, he'd just told me he was leaving at the beginning of summer." Samora had done all he could to ignore this for twenty long years, then one day, through a strange reversal he could not explain to me, he had wanted to give a name, a face, and a story to that long-denied absence. To no avail. It was during that desperate quest that he forged *his new identity*. When I came to Bordeaux, I realized how strange people found it for a black woman to be called Blanche, so I had everyone call me Barbara. Because of her song, the story of a girl who arrives too late to forgive her father. It was because Samora couldn't trace his black origins that he decided to change his name, and he chose the new one in honor of the Mozambican independence leader, Samora Machel, but mainly because his friends had already chosen Madiba and Sankara. He erased the name his mother had given him for good. I kept Blanche for my private life, for love and for sorrow.

I wonder what you will say, the first time you see him. I know you, you'll come out with one of your biting judgmental comments in Kinyarwanda, like the ones you used on me during my childhood, you'll smile and speak to him all the while in your best French. Unless you're sincere. I got the impression, when I saw you last year, that you'd made some concessions, that you'd lost some of the rigidity that used to keep you constantly on your guard in the past. Maybe you understood there was no point in hiding your emotions. You were constantly slipping that proverb into the sermons you delivered, to teach us about life in society: *uguhisha kwakwanga umuhisha kubizi*, if someone hides the fact that he hates you, hide from him the fact you know it. Where did they get us, all those camouflaged feelings? If we'd agreed to look straight at the increasing awkwardness in people's gazes, maybe we would have fled in time. But to go where? All the surrounding countries were already inhabited with thousands of Tutsi who couldn't take another day of their lives in exile. I know, our fate was in the hands of others. And those proverbs were your way, as adults, of masking the fears long hidden beneath a veneer of wisdom. You avoided talking to us about the pogroms of the '60s and '70s. I sometimes try to unravel the skein of our history for Samora; I tell him it's not because we're African that it should be a caricature, that for us, too, it's complicated—all the more so in that, for a century, it was others who read us our fate, who wrote our national story, molded it with clichés and hackneyed myths.

But maybe when I introduce him to you, you'll see in Samora what I immediately sensed: my double, mixed-race like me, stranded on the banks of a river of hypocrisy, the hypocrisy of a century that watched as men—for a night, for a lifetime—loved women who were their exact opposite, then went on home, thoughtless or denying the *collateral damage* that their love of a night, of a lifetime, could cause.

Our father knew them, since he sometimes left the bush where we lived in Ikomoko and walked for a long time to the big town of Butare, for some business he didn't deem worthy of sharing with his children. Our mother, too, for certain, had already seen a few, at least one, since she was the one who would tell us, on nights around the fire, when the dry season had banished the rain along with the mosquitoes and had cleared the sky, making it so bright that, at the far end of the visible earth, we could see the last hills of Ikomoko outlined against a background of twinkling stars, how she thought she would die the first time her gaze ever landed on a *muzungu*. We listened, stunned, while she—usually so sparing of words, to keep our attention riveted since we were tired children ready to squabble—began to weave a tale filled with fear and suspense, which she doled out sparingly by interrupting her story now and again, just long enough to kindle the fire or take a sip of junket. Then she narrowed her eyes and looked beyond the treetops in our plot of land, focused, as if the era she was describing was still lurking in the shadows of the night as it rustled with scary noises. My father was smoking his pipe, leaning against the cob wall of the kitchen, a serene smile on his lips.

"I was already a young woman, old enough to get married, when the deputy chief Rwagatare went around all the homes to order the parents to send their eldest children every afternoon to the chieftancy, starting the very next day, and for three consecutive moons, to do what he called the *Tigisimu*."

Tigisimu: a word she always pronounced in the same manner. I would have to wait until I started secondary school and learned French, a few years later, to come upon the original word which their *native* mouths had transformed: as it changed languages, catechism initially became *Gatigisimu*, then *Tigisimu*, as it went down the social hierarchy.

The king had decreed that young people must go to *Tigisimu*. You could not go against the orders of the King. Worried but obedient parents agreed to let their young ones have their heads filled with this strange thing they were beginning to designate also as *progress*. The deputy chief had warned them that a *muzungu* would be there, but my mother, not knowing what the expression referred to, didn't question her parents at all. In those days, it wasn't done to seem too curious; it was even prohibited by common sense and decency. Just look at the convoluted mannerisms and oratory precautions we still employ before broaching a personal question. I think my generation will have been the first to approach, without shame, the art of questioning the whys and wherefores of the lives of men from here or elsewhere, and not to swallow wholesale the knowledge transmitted by our parents, who had themselves received that knowledge from their parents, without ever questioning any of it—because that would have shown a lack of respect. When I saw the two of you, Blanche and Bosco, coming home from school, your schoolbooks full of question marks at the start of every chapter, which then went on to provide you with the answers—the how and the why of the life of plants, animals, men and their wars—I thought about what my parents' life might have been like if they'd had the same schoolbooks, the same texts, before they were colonized, if they'd been able to master the meaning of the *progress* that had been imposed upon them, without anyone asking them their opinion or even bothering to show them the terms of the contract.

My mother had no idea what a *muzungu* was, and that is why—according to the way she told it to us several years after the fact with many comical details accompanied by exaggerated gestures—she nearly fainted when she saw a little creature wearing a long white robe coming toward the grassy area where they'd been brought together for the *Tigisimu*, because at first she thought he'd been skinned alive.

"His head and eyes and nose and mouth were just like every other human being's, and he had a neck and arms that moved, and surely two legs like ours as well, even though they were hidden beneath a long robe, but he looked like a skinned rabbit, he was as pink as the palms of a newborn's hands! Some of us cried out and ran to find refuge in the little medlar woods along the side of the square where we'd been waiting, seated on the ground. The deputy chief, who had come with the *muzungu*, had to repeat calming words over and over before he could get those girls to come back to our little gathering."

My brothers, my sister, and I heard the story dozens of times, and we always insisted on her telling it, so intrigued were we by this man who had terrified my mother and her schoolmates, even though they were already grown; he seemed more mysterious and frightening than all the wild animals and spirits that inhabited the tales our father sometimes agreed to tell us. Later on, when I was a student at secondary school, where I became used to being with white women every day, I asked her for a few more specific details about the story which had never left my memory: did she remember what year it had been, what the skinned rabbit creature had taught them, what she'd thought about it? But it was one of those days when the few words that came from her mouth seemed like survivors from a long journey through a land of silence, when she had that gaze that could go right through you without seeing you, and she said, "I forget, what do you think he might have told us? He taught us to love *Imana*, God, and to fear him, something our parents had already taught us—but he probably didn't know that."

After that she wouldn't listen to my pleas: "You ask too many questions, it will get you into trouble."

When did I see a white person for the first time? I think Blanche asked me that when she was around ten years old, when she began to understand that my childhood had been vastly different from her own, and that her being of mixed race was more of an accident in the order of things than a story occurring naturally. I clearly remember that I had just started elementary school, so I was six or seven years old. We were at recess, playing on the grassy field outside the school building, which wasn't yet completely finished, when a big black car appeared. I'd already seen one go by in the distance on the road leading to the town, and not only did that metal monster that stirred up as much dust as a herd of terrified cows as it went by not frighten me, it was a source of great fascination. The children and teachers, fearful, didn't budge. Once our initial surprise had passed, some of us even had the same reaction as my mother's schoolmates in the old days: they rushed to hide, some in classrooms, others in the banana plantation behind the school; still others gathered in small silent groups, trembling behind their teachers.

The car door opened, first allowing a pair of shoes to emerge, then two legs covered in dark material, and finally the body of a man, the likes of which we had never seen. A murmur, then a rumble, rose above our unmoving heads, our staring eyes. The school principal silenced us by raising the bamboo stick that never left his hand, always ready to come down on the back of any tardy or recalcitrant pupil. He walked swiftly toward the *muzungu*, his back slightly bent. I was rather upset by the man's appearance, which did not quite match the description our mother had given us: he was not short, nor was he wearing a strange hat on his head, or a white robe over his arms and legs.

So white men came in different shapes and sizes.

He held out his hand to our principal with a smile; the principal took his hand in both of his, which caused a new hubbub among our gang: "He's touching him, look he's touching him, he's going to swallow him!" I don't know where it came from, that belief I'd heard for a long time, even recently from peasants in remote hills like those where I grew up, which drove adults to say to children, "Watch out, the white man is going to eat you, *umuzungu arakurya*!"

The principal invited the *muzungu* visitor into his office and our teachers had to use their sticks to restore a semblance of calm before sending us back to our respective classrooms. When the sound of the car engine could be heard in the courtyard, we all felt a long shiver of excitement go through us, but none of us was bold enough to get up and look out the window with the teacher at the *muzungu* as he drove away.

In the months and years that followed, other white people, in their cars or on foot, appeared more and more often in our daily landscape. The adults knew how to feign polite indifference, while giving them discreet sidelong glances, for I imagine that it was all very strange to them too, but we children, without fail, always had the same reaction. Any vehicle appearing in the distance on the road from Butare was a signal for hordes of kids to rush out of their house, courtyard, field, or pasture to gather at the entrance to what was becoming the business center of Ikomoko and wait for the vehicle to arrive, while conjecturing about its occupants. When they were white, we would crane our necks to try and see their faces, even though, in the opinion of the younger children, they all looked alike, two peas in a pod. Those of us who were a bit older and had a strong stomach dared to run after the car, which invariably slowed down by the bend leading to the mission. The automobiles of the *muzungu* always stopped by the mission. There we remained, clustered together in front of the red spurge bushes, one hand over our mouths in astonishment and admiration; we were just close enough to see the passengers get out, and what they had brought with them—trunks, cardboard suitcases, mysterious instruments—and we were never afraid that we'd be bitten by the dog that was tied up by the door, or that the resident handyman would use his stick, because he was too lazy to come this far to chase us away. When one of the *muzungu*, who could not help but notice what we were up to, started walking toward us, no doubt to say hello, we would panic. We wordlessly took to our heels, the bigger children pushing the others into the spurge bushes, where the sap flowed abundantly from the trampled branches and left indelible stains on our clothes, something our mothers would not fail to punish us for, and severely.

And it was only long after the strangers had gone into the brick building, where none of us had ever set foot, that we resolved to head home and tell the story of what we had seen—throwing in a little exaggeration as a bonus—to all the little scaredy-cats who'd stayed behind.

A new world opened to me the day I began secondary school in Nyanza. Not only did the faculty consist primarily of Westerners, but they were mostly women, and therefore closer to me, at least through their physiognomy.

Everything about these women was a mysterious novelty: their eyes the color of water, their yellow, or thin hair, their smell, which I could not identify with any other known smells. I studied them at length whenever the opportunity arose: in class, the chapel, or the refectory. In the beginning, I always sat as close as possible to one of them to get a better look. All my questions remained unresolved, and I didn't dare ask the other girls, for fear of seeming "weird": were their private parts the same as ours, were their breasts harder, more pointed than ours? What color might their nipples be? One day the biology teacher raised her arms to pin an anatomy poster on the wall, and I saw the hair in her armpits: it was white and curly, even though her face was framed with an austere square of black hair, as fine as the spikelets in the papyrus planted outside the classroom.

My classmates who were from Kigali, Nyundo, or Zaza, where the missions had been founded much earlier, made fun of my fascination with white people, since they had always seen them around.

As the months and years went by, I learned to recognize the things that kept us apart: objects, language, food; but also those that brought us together: laughter, music, lies.

I became a *civilized* young woman, and my mother and father found it hard to recognize me whenever I came home from Nyanza for vacation. They could see that I had changed.

And when, at the end of my studies, I informed them that I didn't intend to come home to live on the hill, they were not surprised, they understood that the new country had completely swallowed me.

It was Léocadie who, the day of our graduation, told me that the Institute of Agronomic Sciences of Rwanda, located in Rubona, not far from Nyanza, was hiring an assistant for one of the Belgian engineers working there. She already had a job set aside for her by her uncle, who was from Gitarama, like Damascène, and was in charge of a department at the MINA-GRI, the Ministry of Agriculture. In those days, young Hutu graduates from the south, above all the ones from Gitarama, president Kayibanda's prefecture, could take their pick when it came to joining the civil service.

I went to see about the position the following week, not having the slightest idea what would be expected of me, wanting only to find a way to leave the family fold. I dreamt about what I would do with my first salary. Like Perrette in the fable by La Fontaine that we had learned in French class, I pictured everything I'd be able to buy with the money I had not yet earned. The security guard I came upon at the entrance to the Institute made me wait for a long time on the one wooden chair with a rock-hard back that was in the dark, silent entrance hall. The sun was already high in the sky, the hot air of the great dry season had made me sweat abundantly as I came up the path on my own from the main road where the bus to Butare had dropped me off. Although the room was cool, and this allowed to me to regain my composure, I felt intimidated. What could I tell these people to convince them to hire me? Léocadie, thanks to her uncle, had got me an informational brochure about the Institute, which I had learned by heart the night before. I knew it had been founded in 1962, not long after independence, in order to continue, on the Rwandan side, the work carried out since the '30s by the National Institute for Agronomic Study of the Belgian Congo. I knew it was in charge of "agro-sylvo-pastoral" research, with a view to "improving production and living conditions for a peasantry that has often been victim to famine due to erosion, unfamiliarity with modern techniques of breeding and agriculture, and also overpopulation." I had painstakingly checked the spelling of any word I thought I might have to know for the dictation I imagined they would give me to verify my mastery of French. My brand-new diploma was waiting in a big manila envelope to be waved before anyone who wanted to make sure I'd been a good, obedient, hard-working student.

The security guard seemed to have forgotten me, and I was afraid that he'd fallen asleep beneath his cap. I thought about asking him again if someone could receive me, when I heard determined steps crunching the gravel in the courtyard. I leapt to my feet when I saw that the employee, who had also stood up straight, pointed me out to a little *muzungu* wearing khaki shorts and a white short-sleeved shirt. The man didn't take the time to listen to everything the other man was saying to him. He came into the hall and, without stopping, asked me to go with him. I hurried to follow close behind. I think that that was the day I picked up the habit of going everywhere at a near-run, that fast clip which you described as being neither feminine nor Rwandan, and which I forbade Blanche from imitating. Monsieur Herbillon, that was his name, didn't subject me to an interview. He glanced distractedly at the diploma I held out. Here I had thought I was going to be evaluated on the strength of my French, my typing skills, all those *Western* things I had just spent six years studying assiduously, so I was disconcerted when he placed before me a wooden board that was covered with dried beans.

"Do you know what these are? Did your parents teach you how to grow things before sending you to secondary school, my little friend?"

He always called me "my little friend." I found it a little humiliating and strange, until the day Antoine explained to me that it was affectionate, that older people did that back where they came from. The old man must have been in his fifties, he was thin and bald, and always wore a tired smile, which attenuated the hardness of his face with its prominent cheekbones. I looked at the beans, hesitated, then answered all in a rush, pointing at them with a trembling finger, mentally blessing my father for his eagerness to teach his children everything he knew, both at home and in the fields:

"This one is an *umubano*, that one is the *urunyumba* and finally this one I think they call it *ngwinurare*." Then I looked up at him, waiting for the verdict.

"Very good. You can start on Monday. Where do you live?"

I couldn't get over it. It had been so easy.

My voice emerged in a faint croak, "I live with my parents

in Ikomoko, but I'm going to look for lodgings in Butare, to be closer."

"Perfect. I live there too, I can give you a lift to and from work. Get in touch with the procurator's office and tell them I sent you, I know they have a home for young women near the cathedral, you can find a cheap room to rent there. I'll expect you on Monday at eight A.M., don't be late, will you, my little friend."

He handed me a book with a black cover. "Here, I don't know what your biology teacher told you about plants. You have two days to read this little manual, otherwise you won't understand a thing about what I'll be asking you to do."

He didn't leave me the time to thank him. He went out of his office through a different door than the one we had used to come in, and he left it open. As he walked past the passion-flower covering the white-washed walls on the way to his car, it trembled in his wake.

The following Saturday, I moved to Butare. Every morning we would head off in his little truck to various regions in the south of the country: sometimes we had to collect plants in the Nyungwe Forest where the Institute was conducting studies about the conservation and exploitation of natural forests. They provided me with boots, and I had my first pair of trousers made. On other days we went to meet with farmers who gathered at their cooperative for informational sessions about the new *seeds* and growing techniques the Institute wanted to disseminate on every hill. I saw to the translation. Monsieur Herbillon had been living in the region for a long time. Before Rwanda, he'd worked for the Agronomical and Zootechnical Research Institute at Gitega in Burundi, but he couldn't say more than ten words in our language.

The farmers looked skeptically at this very young woman who sometimes stammered, but remained focused, eager not to misconstrue what the white man said, taking care all the while to keep the scientific terms accessible, along with the injunctions to change that poured from her boss's thin lips. They must have been wondering how a mouth with so little flesh on it could contain so many words, dry words or round words you'd have to pronounce holding your nose, mysterious words whose meaning they tried to guess by looking at the *muzungu*'s squinting eyes. No doubt they also found it strange that this representative of the West—which, so he told them, had developed very efficient farming techniques and whose granaries were overflowing with a wealth of food—could be so thin, and they must have concluded that he could not be completely honest.

In the evening I was too tired to walk around Butare, which I barely knew. And in any case, the students were on vacation, the expatriates had gone to their summer quarters back in their own country, and the city seemed to be sleeping; only when mass let out on Sundays was a semblance of liveliness restored to the clean, quiet streets.

The other lodgers at the home for young women explained to me that two masses were held at the cathedral: one early in the morning for the maids, workers, and peasants from the surrounding area, and one at midday which the *enlightened* people attended, some of them coming on their motorcycles or bikes, or even by car. As I'd studied, and was now a working girl, I was not going to lower myself by attending the early mass. I could at last indulge in the delight of sleeping in, and take my time to make myself pretty before going to the ten o'clock mass. Who knew, maybe I would meet a young civil servant there who'd be a good match, the way the previous occupant of my room had done? It had been over a year since your father Damascène had gone away across the ocean, and he hadn't written me a single letter.

BLANCHE

July, 1997. Three years after fleeing the genocide, I was back in Butare. I was home. I said "Odi," then stepped timidly toward Bosco. He put his arms around me. A sigh ran through our chests, pressed close together. Then he held me at arm's length, a familiar little gesture, the better to look at me. He'd begun to do this when he was fifteen, once he had grown taller than me. My huge little brother had rounded shoulders and a slouching back. His eyes conveyed nothing beyond astonishment. His fingers closed around my arms, so hard it hurt; a moment later he suddenly let go. An automatic little pat on the cheek, like a muted slap, or a blessing that had landed in the wrong place; his hands were cool. He still hadn't said a word, I had a catch in my throat. The lid of sorrow was about to be lifted.

It was just then that you appeared, Mama, in the doorway leading into the corridor. You let out a long cry, you cried out because I was there. It was neither joy nor surprise, it was something deeper and more animal than I'd ever heard. You flung yourself at me, or rather between Bosco and me, as if you wanted to separate us, to prevent an imminent crime.

You folded me in your thin arms, you pressed your cheek, already damp, against my buzzing ear. A young woman I didn't know, probably the maid, ran into the room, alarmed by your cry, and it spoiled the magic of the moment. I could see her bare feet, very wide, with toes obscenely spread, leaving damp prints on the reddish cement floor. I would have liked to feel the coolness of that floor rise up my back and ease the pain that was paralyzing my body.

Bosco stepped to one side and stood at the end of the living room, the already absent spectator of a wordless scene; he remained impassive at the sight of our red, tearful eyes.

"Mama, let her sit down, can't you see she looks like she's about to collapse."

"Yes, you're right." You always thought he was right about everything.

You lifted up a fold of your pagne, which was loosely tied over a faded dress that was too big for you, to wipe your face, and you forced me to sit down in a wooden armchair without a cushion. I wondered what had become of all our furniture. It had probably been looted. The living room was practically empty. Four chairs, a coffee table and, in a corner, a chest with glass doors. Crocheted doilies everywhere. Those, I recognized. It was my grandmother who'd made them. She'd always had a project in her hand, she liked bright colors and geometric shapes. If she could have seen us just then . . .

A family in need of mending.

"*Mwana wanjye ni wowe?* Is that you, my child?"

Your voice was low, extremely hoarse. I realized you'd begun smoking again.

I could see a patch of sky through the front door. The sun was at its zenith now, causing white rays to stream down the brick wall and splash onto the plants. In concrete planters, tall canna indica were growing, yellow and red, and boatlilies. They were making the most of the meager shade of a young banana plant that hadn't been there before. The courtyard seemed much smaller than in the memory I'd fashioned in exile. The living room, too, seemed small and shabby. Nostalgia idealizes things.

The maid couldn't take her eyes off me, she must have seen pictures of me, did she know who I was? You didn't let go of my hands, you seemed to be waiting for me to say something.

Mentally I'd prepared a list of sentences I thought would suit various scenarios. Hypothesis number 1: you get angry because I didn't tell you I was coming, I get everything off my chest all at once, then I leave you there, free of the burden of my resentment. Hypothesis number 2: you weep with joy and tell me how much you've missed me, you ask me never to go away again, I take the time to reassure you, make the most of the joy of being together again, and wait for the right moment to bring up the past. Hypothesis number 3: you have lied to me about your health, you are suffering from the serious physical after-effects of the genocide, I persuade you to come back to France with me, and I get in touch with Samora to prepare your hospitalization in Bordeaux.

I thought I'd mapped everything out in the airplane bringing me home.

You can't map out a collapse.

I didn't know what sort of attitude to adopt. Your lips were smiling but the sadness in your eyes was unfathomable. In my anxious predictions I hadn't factored in Bosco's presence. How could I have erased him? And yet I knew he'd come back, that he'd been living at home since his return from the front. As if this story was only about you and me, Mama; you and me.

He was there between us, the way he'd always been.

You were both waiting for me to speak. I was the one who'd left, I was the one who had to pick up the thread of the conversation, to let you know where we'd left off. Set the pace. In my head, the words I'd prepared were not up to the task, they didn't make sense anymore, fled against the current. The little maid had slipped discreetly out of the room, and a thick, sticky silence was forming around us again. How did we speak to one another, before? I seemed to have forgotten. Which *before* did I want to return to, anyway? There were two of them. No, three.

Was it the before of the first of October, 1990, and the beginning of the civil war, and before you were thrown in jail with everyone the government accused of being *ibyitsos*, traitors in cahoots with their exiled Tutsi brothers who had attacked the country, until you returned six months later, fear frozen in your body?

Was it the before of 1991, and Bosco's departure for the front? His sudden disappearance, our failure to understand until we received a note, passed on clandestinely, which said, "I've joined my father's friends, get ready, we're coming," and which only increased your fear, Mama?

We had stayed alone, waiting for him, trying to fill the void caused by the detonation of his absence with the prayers and hymns he liked. We spoke less and less.

Or was it the before of April, 1994, before I fled from Butare, where the genocide had not yet begun, but when everywhere else in the country they were wielding their machetes, and you entrusted me to a convoy of expats being evacuated by the Belgian army to Burundi? Then you had no one left to talk to.

Three "befores," three and a half years for it all to fall apart, a headlong rush into the future toward the disaster we didn't want to see coming. We went through those troubled times not knowing how to name them. Everyone in Butare was going around saying, "There's an evil wind blowing," *hari umwuka mubi*, but as winds go, it was a hurricane that was about to come down upon us.

How did the three of us use to talk together, when the breeze was still light? Before. Wouldn't it have been incongruous to speak to you the way I did before? I was certainly the one who'd been best protected through what the world referred to as "a tragedy." A tragedy, as if it were inevitable. It suits them well, in the world, to think there was nothing to be done, that the die was cast from the beginning, because in places like that, don't you know, they've been killing each other since the dawn of time. I was alone that day at noon, standing there before the two of you, and the world still didn't want to hear the infinite echo of those three years in our lives. I would have liked to patch us back together with my lips, find soothing words, gentle gestures, above all nothing that would upset you. I put away my spite, the story of my father, my exile, all my struggles in France. What you and Bosco had been through was incommensurable.

I gave a faint smile, and squeezed your hands in return.

"I've finished my studies, I could come and see you at last. I've missed you." There I was, going and making excuses for myself again, trying to obtain forgiveness. For what? Not coming sooner? And yet on the telephone you had said, "Stay there, live your life, protect yourself from sorrow, here we spend weeks digging up bones and giving them the dignity of a decent burial, the schools aren't really functioning yet; for those of us who survived, life is bitter, so much has been buried. You have a home at last. You'll come see us when the country and people's hearts have been repaired."

The country would get back on its feet, of that I had no doubt, even if it took thirty years. There would be the manpower, the determination of all those who had dreamt about it from far away for three decades, the guilt of those who had destroyed it, and the guilt of the world that had let them, the unprecedented motivation the survivors would find in themselves to forge ahead and offer a new horizon for the children they would have. But hearts cannot be repaired the way a roof can, or a road, or a city razed to the ground. If I'd had to wait for my mother's heart to go back to the exact same place where it was at rest, intact once again (had it ever really been intact?), I would have had to resign myself to never setting foot in Butare again.

Unless I apologized for being there today? Since I hadn't gone through any of it, and I couldn't know and never would really know what you had been through. My childhood melancholy at being torn from my country, however deep it might have been, could not show me the measure of your nostalgia for humanity. Like you, I had wept over the loss of my cousins, my grandfather, my uncles and their wives, my friends; but you had seen them dying, mutilated, you had searched for their remains for months on end and then you buried them. Where had I been all that time? For me, life had gone on.

"We missed you, too." Bosco came to sit next to us and placed his hands on ours. A shared silence fell over us, and guilt evaporated.

Our hearts meeting, in tatters.

When I think back on that scene in the living room last summer, my throat feels so tight it could explode. I'd been throwing up all day long, Samora wanted to call the doctor but I talked him out of it. There was nothing he could do for me, I just had to take in the news, digest it and let it spread all through my limbs. We came home that morning from the maternity clinic. Samora's features were drawn, I thought, wasn't that just typical of a man, to be tired when I was the one who'd done all the work, tired now that I really needed him. Stokely was feeding every two or three hours, he had colic and was crying a lot. I was sleeping in fits and starts.

Samora waited for me to feed him, waited until he'd changed him and got him to sleep in his basket, before he spoke.

"I finally managed to reach someone from your family last night."

I didn't like his serious tone, I could feel a quiver in my gut.

He had never said "someone from your family" before, he liked to say "Rwanda," rounding his lips greedily like when he said "my love." But now he seemed to be driving some phantom word away with his pinched lips.

"Did you talk to my mother? Why didn't you tell me earlier? What's going on, is she not well? Tell me, go on, tell me!"

"Your brother died."

Nothing could have prepared me for that.

Between 1991 and 1994, we dreaded it every day, our souls unquiet, our dreams deferred. But Bosco had come back from the war alive, without any wounds anyone could see. Ravaged, lost, walled up inside himself, but alive. How could he be dead, now that peace had returned?

"When did he die? Who killed him?" I couldn't stay silent. The news had set off a shrill whistling in my head, constant, invading me from inside, and I thought that speaking would alleviate it.

"I think it was the day after Stokely was born. I don't know how he died."

"You think? What do you mean, you don't know, you didn't ask my mother? You didn't think it concerned you, or you forgot, how can this be?" I was raising my voice, shooting daggers at him, my rage increasing, the storm approaching, I was about to explode.

He knelt down beside me. Samora understood that my rage wasn't against him. Awkwardly, he tried to calm me down.

"I wasn't able to get your mother in person. Your aunt told me, ever since she found Bosco's body in the living room, your mother has been mute. She didn't want to tell me what killed him. I'm really sorry, I can imagine how devastated you must feel."

In the living room? His body laid out in the living room,

our living room? I was besieged with images of the three of us in that room during my visit the year before. At the time I was already pregnant with Stokely, but I didn't know. I felt nauseous but I thought it was from all the emotion—my painful return, the halting words exchanged with my brother. Halting, yes, we could no longer feel the gentle closeness of kinship. There was a barrier of seven years between us: his two wars, first in Rwanda then in Zaire; my defection to France. Which he held against me. Already the morning after I arrived, there were these words he spat out, as if they'd been in his mouth for too long:

"What you guys did—"

"What do you mean, 'you guys'?"

And you, Mama, panicking, "Leave her alone, you know it's no fault of hers!"

"I mean her people, you have their blood in you, and their nationality, don't you?"

And me, defensive, "The French people had no way of knowing what their president and their ministers and their army were doing."

"It's your money, they came with weapons, your money financed the militias and bought their weapons."

Already the second day, doors slamming, a silence full of unsaid reproach. Mama, I haven't forgotten that you begged him never to speak of it ever again. He started smoking, that man who'd always criticized you for your addiction. He was constantly over at the cabaret, going to bed late, incapable of getting up before noon. We would meet in the living room for a lunch of few words and food that tasted of tears. Our happy reunion blown to smithereens.

Toward the end, there was an attempt at mending: *Tell me about your life there, will you make a good living? Do you think you'll ever come back here to live?* I told him about Samora. *That's good, you'll be able to give Mama some grandchildren.* I haven't dared to tell her yet, she might worry. *Why, aren't you going to get married?* I don't know yet, people there live together without getting married. *Do you already live together?* Yes. *Then you have to get married, don't have a baby like that, it would kill her.* How is she, do you sometimes talk about what happened? *I haven't dared to ask her much about it, I think she sensed I was afraid of it.*

Bosco told me:

"I was the one who found her, you know, when we took the city on July 3, 1994. She had just come out of her hiding place in the bookstore. Three months in that hole underground, the killers didn't even know what a basement was, the imbeciles. Mind you, I didn't either, it's a white thing, we don't have them here. She could've spent years in there. When I found her, she hadn't eaten in a week. The man who'd been feeding her fled with the other Hutus when we reached the edge of the town. He just left her a little jug of water and three bananas. She was so thin, if you'd seen her, she hadn't washed her hair since April, and it was sticking straight up on her head, she had this mad look in her eyes, I almost didn't recognize her. She had dragged herself to the door of the wrecked bookstore, she was prepared to hand herself over to the killers rather than rot in the basement. If I'd come one day later, I wouldn't have found her alive, you know. You know the walls were covered with cockroaches? I got there before she was doomed once and for all. The irony of it. *Inyenzi muzindi nyenzi*, a cockroach among the cockroaches. They would have eaten her body. The door to the bookstore was locked, the man who'd been hiding her had forgotten to give her the key before he fled to Zaire. She saw us through a hole in the wood. Soldiers wearing tall black rubber boots. She picked up a brick that was on the floor and banged on the door with all the strength she had left. Her voice was too weak to call out. Her banging was drowned out by the sound of our boots parading down the main street. She banged for a long time.

"I had to feed her with a spoon those first days, as if she were a baby. We didn't have much to eat, I gave her my daily ration, she talked and talked and wept the minute she recognized someone, from her mat in the shed where we'd put the survivors. Every time she came upon someone she knew, it was like a miracle. She asked for news of what had happened in this or that neighborhood, who'd been killed, when, who by. Mama had been hidden all that time, you know, she'd heard the noise, sometimes shouts, gunshots, but she didn't see anything. In the evening when I came back to see her, she wanted to tell me everything, who'd been killed and when and who by and in the most horrible way. I didn't have the courage to listen to all those stories she was coming out with, it was exhausting. I had just walked across a country littered with decomposing corpses, from Kagitumba to Butare, from the north to the south. Do you know how many gutted houses, mass graves, churches full of crushed skulls we saw? From Kagitumba to Butare, from the north to the south, the same skeletons, arms held out to us with their last spared breath, the same women walking unsteadily. The gazes of women who'd been raped, fleeing the humiliation of their bodies ravaged by monsters with poisoned genitals, dozens, thousands of them. The same purulent stumps under homemade bandages, holes in their foreheads, torn cheeks, and me, you know, I'd been a soldier, brave in combat, but I had no tears left to sob with them. I couldn't stomach it, the catastrophe there before our eyes. *Amagara araseseka ntayorwa.* Spilled guts can't be picked up, as the ancestors said. And wherever we stopped, from Kagitumba to Butare, from the north to the south, I imagined our mother's face behind every dead or living woman I came upon, in a hole, behind a door. I had to remain stoical, while all around me everything had gone to pieces. I wanted to run away, I thought about deserting, you know, to cross the country at night, to come and get her, but I knew the fate they held in store for deserters. If she'd survived, Mama would need a son who was alive. Not one gunned down by a firing squad.

"So when I found her, I couldn't stand that incontinent flow of words—who'd been killed in Butare by who and when and where and in what horrible way, over and over and over again, you see, I'd already seen too much and heard too much. Aunt Maria and her grandchildren came back from Burundi, they'd managed to get there with the convoy from Terre des Hommes, on June 18, from the school in Karubanda where they'd survived, miraculously. I moved them into our house. Everything had been looted so I went and helped myself in turn from the houses of Hutus who'd fled. After that, I returned to the fighting in the north, where everything had begun. We still had to liberate Ruhengeri and Gisenyi.

"I came back often, I wanted to make sure they were doing okay. When Mama was able to walk, they would go and hunt for news, survivors, the bodies of Maria's children, of their father and brothers, of all our family members. They spent a whole year, you know, looking and burying, looking and weeping. Then they asked to go and spend a week in Tanzania, just so they could get a change of scene, see something besides death. That's when I called you, remember, so that you'd help me pay for the first vacation they'd ever had in their life. They told me they slept for a whole week nonstop, they only got up to eat and wash. When they got home, Mama and Auntie opened the restaurant again. They had to find the money to send the grandchildren to school, to return, reluctantly, to life—for them, the next generation.

"We never spoke openly about the genocide again. Mama understood that I didn't have the strength to listen to her anymore. But I think it's there in their conversation at every moment. They're stuck in those hundred days. They'll never get out, they were too old when it happened."

He fell silent, but sat with his mouth agape as if he were frozen in a stupor. Bosco had never confided in me this much before, Mama, you know; he had just come out with it all in one go, the way you drain a glass after a long arid trip or a sorrowful dawn nightmare. He never spoke to me that way again, but at the time, I didn't know he wouldn't have the strength to live with his own demons for much longer. He told me almost nothing about them.

"And you, Bosco, how are you? I'm sorry about your fiancée, I'm so sorry."

"Yes, *aho umutindi yanitse ntiriva.* Fate always pursues the wretched."

For a long moment he didn't speak, after he'd uttered that maxim in a muffled voice.

Then he continued in the same monotone, to tell me what had happened. He and his fiancée had already set the date for the wedding. He'd met her at the front. A wartime love that had survived the end of illusions. Her family had some difficulty with the idea she'd be marrying a half-Hutu, the brother of a Frenchwoman on top of it, but he'd earned his stripes in the army and she was prepared to fall out with them in order to marry him, she sincerely loved him, and her parents eventually gave in. Fate decided otherwise. It was a white man who crushed her: "One of those vultures, come to make money off our misery in the name of humanitarianism. One of your lot, Belgian or Swiss, I don't know anymore." I could have let that last comment go, agreed to be relegated yet again to a side I hadn't chosen, the side of all my skin-color-half-brothers, colonialists and other whites from the beginning of time. But I spoke out: "Stop always putting me with the bad guys, please."

The confession came to an abrupt halt, and Bosco left me there without further ado. He only came back in the middle of the night. The next day I flew back to Bordeaux.

I still can't believe he's dead now. And that there are people who think I had something to do with it. Do you believe that, Mama? Why won't you speak to me? He was your favorite child, I always suspected as much, but to refuse to speak to me, aren't you punishing me unfairly? I'm your only living child now. You refuse to speak to me and I sit here writing these letters to you that I don't send. That's what we've become. Sometimes I think it was inevitable. This failure to communicate.

Aunt Maria told me Bosco killed himself. That you found him still warm, his shattered head in an ashtray. She told me not to tell anyone. Who would you have me tell, here, I hardly know any Rwandans. Never utter that shameful word, suicide. "It is a very great sin, my child, no one must know."

"Why did he do it, Auntie?"

"God alone knows that. But you see, after your departure, he wasn't well."

"My departure, Auntie! You mean our argument the day of my departure had something to do with it, the business about the house? I hope that's not what you're implying!"

Silence on the line.

"No, of course not, it wasn't just that, he wasn't the same after the war anyway, especially after he came back from Zaire, but your argument certainly drove him deeper."

"Look, Mama must have told you, he wanted to force me to sign a paper where I would have left him all the rights to the house, the restaurant, the shop, everything! It belonged to my father, that's the only thing I have from him, I wasn't about to sign. And given how unstable he was, he was perfectly capable of selling it all for a bottle of gin or a carton of cigarettes, and at that rate, Mama would have ended up out on the street in no time. You think I should have gone along with it, is that what you think, Maria, really?"

"No, of course not, you did the right thing, it's true it was your inheritance. Bosco's father didn't leave him a thing, he didn't even know he existed."

"But I don't care about property, if someone could bring Bosco back to life, I would immediately give him everything I own, it's not that business that was driving him crazy, it can't be, Mama would have told me, she didn't say anything about it on the phone these last months, she didn't even tell me things had gotten worse with him, why didn't she say something?"

"She knew you were pregnant, she didn't want to upset you. She said that when you argued, you said hurtful things, she said, 'When she comes back, I'll tell her to apologize to her brother, I'll reconcile them, I'll tell them the whole story about their fathers at last, I'll ask Blanche to forgive me and I'll repair their hearts.'"

Gusana imitima, repair hearts.

Bosco's heart has stopped beating. What a waste, what a waste, Mama. Never again will the three of us be there in the living room, never again our stories out on that little bench under the jacaranda trees. Our family in shreds.

Someday we'll come and you'll meet your grandson, Stokely, and I hope you'll find your language as a mother again, to explain this proverb to him, one you taught me: "*Agahinda nti-kica kagira mubi*, grief does not kill, it damages." And anyway, is that the right translation? Is it "it damages" or "it makes a person bad"? I don't know anymore, I don't know. Grief swept everything away, and it took Bosco, my immense little brother, who made it back from the war, without any wounds anyone could see.

Why do we still say "mother tongue?" It made sense when mothers stayed at home alone feeding their infant with sounds to guide it toward its first babbling; when the mothers of mothers and their aunts and sisters made up a chorus of voices, fluttering birds, prisoners of the women's quarters, caressing the child's ears with wings made of drawings, colors constantly whirling. The intonations: iridescent circles; the accents: symmetrical streaks, the "clicks" above, the rolling below. The child learned to weave a link of sound between the pointing finger and the object that was still blurry to its eyes, between laughter and its origin, learned to differentiate between the calm silence peopled with onomatopoeia of restfulness in "phew: the work is done," and the heavy silence of reproof or pique that accompanied the "tchip" of sucked teeth, pouting lips, frowning brows.

Night birds in the middle of the day.

For Stokely's mother, it wasn't like that. When the father and mother don't share the same mother tongue, which language carries the day?

Blanche only sampled her mother's language by accident. For want of anything better. Immaculata hadn't planned it that way; to liberate her daughter from her Africanness, she braided her a ladder of very white words. Right from her birth her daughter had been plunged into a bath of French, and the mother never allowed herself to slip up with an indigenous expression. The father, who had never mastered any language

other than that of Molière—to his regret—did suggest, however, that she give the little girl some keys to the local parlance:
"Let her hear Kinyarwanda, she's going to grow up here and,
who knows, maybe one day she'll get married here." This even-
tuality terrified the mother, for it was not without difficulty
that she'd managed to rise above her own condition: it would
be out of the question for her child to backslide, and take the
others with her, by loving someone as black as she was.
Blanche must be true to her name, must speak perfect French
and later, why not, English too, to go and see America, but
under no circumstances must she acquire the means to communicate with the servants, who risked contaminating her with
their backward ideas. If the girl didn't understand the lower
classes, it would save her from damnation—from life on the
hill, under the sun and under the same rain, unchanging, century upon century. And never mind if that also cut her off from
her grandfather's sharp wisdom, or her grandmother's pithy
proverbs. In any event, as soon as she was of age—it had
already been decided—she would go and continue her studies
in France, to perfect her accent and her cultural knowledge,
and to marry a real white man with whom, to her mother's
great delight, she would conceive descendants, who would be
increasingly diluted.

These plans, like so many others, ended up in the cemetery
of Immaculata's dreams. When Blanche was old enough to say
her first words, neither her father nor her mother were by her
side. When Immaculata got out of prison, she went to find her
child who, for several months, had been cuddled, consoled,
and tucked in at night by her grandmother and her aunt, and
was now perfectly at ease with the native parlance. The mother
swallowed her pride and her imported language at the same
time; fate had punished her for being too ambitious. And thus,
Blanche settled into the idiom of her gut and her heart, the one

that came from the depths of childhood. And, perfectly logically, Kinyarwanda would soon become the language with which to welcome Bosco into the world, Bosco who would be born even darker than his mother. Whiteness was no longer a given horizon; it was just a faint possibility in the future, like winning the jackpot at a raffle, or eternal peace.

The day Immaculata went to enroll her daughter in the Albert Camus kindergarten in Butare, still wrapped in a weave of outdated pride (had she not, for two whole years, been the legitimate spouse of a member of that expatriate community?), she nearly died of shame when she learned that Blanche would be taking remedial classes in French, along with a handful of children from affluent Rwandan families who attended the school. She nearly threatened the headmistress with sending Blanche to the nearby Belgian school, but didn't, bitterly contemplating her fall from grace and France's failure to keep its promises, brought home to her by the tricolor flag reproduced on Blanche's birth certificate from the French Embassy.

After six months had gone by, the little girl was perfectly bilingual. Her mother regained hope. Hesitating between rebuilding her ruins and living in them, Immaculata now made a point of honor, whenever she was in company, to speak to her daughter exclusively in her father's language, reserving her own idiom for the privacy of home and her patchwork family.

To Blanche, French became an injunction, a decorative veneer that sounded odd in the presence of strangers, who looked at her with respect. A yoke of a language she only cast off when wings took her to the heart of nursery rhymes, of children's songs, then later, opened the windows into books, gave access to symbols of a centuries-old collective memory shared by women and men like her father. She looked for him in every description of a clear gaze, of an adventurous life, of a thwarted paternal love. This man who had vanished, who had never written to her, would wear the garments of fictional heroes, of mythical absent fathers, become a fantasy, adopting a voice and an intonation with a reassuring, familiar lilt. Yes, that was it, and one day she would read a sentence that confirmed what she felt: books could bring *closeness, complicity, or better still, beyond that, a long-lost kinship found at last.*

To Blanche, French could be both a delightful, solitary thing, and a public corset, ridiculous and pretentious.

As for her mother tongue, it was her backbone, the language in which she expressed her sorrows and kept her secrets, the language in which she could argue with Bosco, be scolded by their mother, or experience the atmosphere of a fiery Sunday on Butare's main street when the *Mukura* football team had won.

To own two languages completely is to be hybrid, to carry two souls within, each one cloaked in a cape of interlaced words, an outfit to wear according to context, and whose cut defines the limits of expressible feeling. Inhabiting two parallel worlds, each one rich with treasures that others cannot even suspect; but also, constantly, living on the border.

When she was ten, and she began to write to her absent father, letters she hid in the false ceiling in her room. French took on new colors and burgundy threads of velvet, birds of stolen words.

But after her baccalaureate exam, it became clear that her father still did not intend to write to her and would not be welcoming his daughter to that dreamt-of country. Blanche stopped writing to him and forgot about the letters she had never sent, which now formed four collapsing towers under the roof of the house; she was like a spurned fiancée who abandons her trousseau embroidery beneath a dust of dried-up sighs. Crucified birds.

By that time, Immaculata only spoke to her daughter in Kinyarwanda. The outlook had never been bleaker. All that was left were novels: elsewhere, within the range of words. Madame Bovary, or Zola's Gervaise, still weeping for their decline, in French.

The mother's last injunction before Blanche climbed into the convoy evacuating Butare's Westerners, at the beginning of the genocide, was this, however, "With every militia or soldier or Black man you meet between here and the border, be true to your name, whiter than ever. Forget my language, where you're headed, it will be nothing more than a useless burden. Go, become French, my child."

And yet, four months later, when she called Blanche from Kigali to tell her, "I'm alive," she spoke to her daughter only in Kinyarwanda. The phone lines were still down in Butare, she'd ridden in a ramshackle pick-up truck along a road full of land-mines to be able to speak to her. Later, thinking back, Blanche reasoned that if her mother was calling her from a public place, it must have seemed wise not to use the idiom of the country that had supported the deposed murderous regime. She began to cherish her language from back there, nostalgia-birds, all the more so in that she was afraid she would lose her mastery of the words strewn like so many little pebbles scattered in vain along the one-way road to exile.

So, when she gave birth to Stokely, she thought, "This child's been born with a frenulum under his tongue, he'll have to be given, shamelessly and directly, two loose, silky garments, to cross the north and south of his destiny harmoniously." Colorful birds.

Samora, who had made several fruitless attempts as an out-sider to learn his father's Creole, had encouraged her from the moment they knew she was pregnant; it was an era when, at the bookstore, you could easily find recordings of lullabies from

Africa, some of which were in Kinyarwanda. The unborn child bathed in them. Every night, its mother would sing to the little feet drumming on the taut skin of her belly, songs nestled in her memory, treasures she had safeguarded from the time of evenings on the bench by the jacarandas.

Stokely was born, Bosco died. Immaculata became mute. For the first time, Blanche lost her nerve. What was the point of this language, if it could not get past some blockage in her mother's throat that was stifling her with grief? What was the point of teaching this language, with everything it evoked in the way of sorrow, to an innocent child who hadn't asked for any of it? Did she express her secret hope that the voice of this grandson, speaking to his grandmother with the words she had once taught her son Bosco, would act as a balm—rhizome words—for Immaculata? Blanche tried to go on naming animals, objects, food; to go on singing. But she had to give up, more and more often, when she found herself confessing to her son in French, "I don't know how to say 'giraffe,' I never saw any, the park was on the other side of the country, my mother could tell me, but you know she's put a padlock on her mouth and thrown the key away."

Or, "There's no word for 'fox,' or 'bear' or 'sea lion,' they don't exist back where we come from." Stokely would suck on his rattle, indifferent to the ordeals of translation his mother was going through.

Then, as if after a long landslide, the French resurfaced, the ease of words which spring to mind, the momentum of conversations with others that make one forget. Blanche was unable to sew on her own the garment of imported words. Before long, the mother had stopped speaking her mother tongue to her son, except in rare bursts when, overcome by strong emotion, anger or fear, she shouted without thinking, things like "*ceceka*, shut up," or "*ngwino hano*, come here."

Slightly ashamed for having given up, she would reassure

Samora by saying, "When we go there, we'll be immersed in it, and he'll learn incredibly fast."

The only little island that was never covered over by the wave of French was the moment for bedtime, when it was all *ndagukunda*, I love you, calming little drums, the different ways of saying good night, almost all tinged with an ancestral fear of the evil lurking in the dark: *urare aharyana*—sleep where it itches so you'll remain vigilant; *uramuke*—may you survive the night; *uraran'Imana*—may God protect your sleep. And always, always the song that she and Immaculata used to listen to over and over, before the genocide, hoping for Bosco's return:

Muvandimwe wanjye Ubalijoro, uraho uracyakomaho
My brother Ubalijoro, are you still alive?
Natwe ino ngaho turaho, uretse ko tutazi agakuru kawe
Here we are fine, but have no news of you
Uzagire ugaruke Ubalijoro, twese uko tuli turagukumbuye
Please come back Ubalijoro, we all miss you so
I Buganda n'iyo haba heza hate, rwose nta gihugu cyaruta Urwanda
However beautiful Uganda might be, no country is the equal of Rwanda
Haherutse kuza inkuru itubwira, ko ngo iyo uba habaye intambara
We heard that war broke out there, where you're living now
Abantu ngo bakwiriye imishwaro, wowe se aho yaragusize?
That people scattered as they fled, did you survive the war?
Niba se ukiriho Ubalijoro, rwose twandikire dushire intimba
And if you're still alive, Ubalijoro, write to ease our sorrow
Uzagire ugaruke Ubalijoro, twese uko tuli turagukumbuye.
Please come back, Ubalijoro, we all miss you so.

Blanche had convinced herself she wouldn't abandon her

intention to teach Stokely her language, that she was just putting it off until later. Without realizing, she passed on all the
body language from her own upbringing: the disapproving
gaze that makes you stop in your tracks—*kureba ijisho*, discre-
tion as a way of life, don't let anything show, stay polite and
humble at all times, discreetly rubbing your fingernail—*kurya
urwara* to interrupt a child carelessly chattering with an adult
who's too curious. The art of subtly changing the subject of
conversation so that the other person doesn't realize the confession of a secret has just been nipped in the bud. And then
that word she said to him over and over, a unique word that
summed up all the instructions, the intransigent path toward a
child's autonomy: "*ibwirize*," do what you're supposed to do
without us having to ask you. Samora thought his wife was too
strict. Blanche stood her ground: if it all starts again someday
in the future, if one day he has to go through anything like
what I endured, I want him to be mature and able to show, no
matter the circumstances, the utmost courtesy. To be accepted
by whoever takes him in, to blend into any mold, without ever
forgetting his culture or where we come from.

When he was three years old, Stokely and his mother didn't
talk all that much to each other: she couldn't understand this
thing that Westerners had of drowning their children beneath
a flood of explanations, constantly addressing them as if they
were little scholars. Stokely never asked that many questions to
begin with, and he could spend an entire hour just watching
ants or pigeons, listening to music, playing with his Playmobil,
leafing through an herbarium, absorbing images, inventing terrifying stories, all without turning to his parents. The boy loved
his mother's characteristic Rwandan noises to communicate:
the "tchip," that could be short and curt, or long and lethal;
the clicking of her tongue at the back of her palate, the way she
slapped her thigh when she couldn't stop laughing, or clapped

her hands to congratulate herself for telling a good joke. All these gestures brought them closer and prepared their hearts for the words they'd give each other later on, the settled words they'd share when the time came. Stokely understood that his mother had ghost words inside her, childhood words that had fallen asleep in a garden lying fallow, which a distant rain might revive someday. Birds of life.

IMMACULATA

hildren keep you alive. You saved me from the madness of men. As long as I didn't know what had become of you, and I didn't know if you'd survived, a superhuman force compelled me to fight. I endured hiding in a damp hole infested with cockroaches, underground as they were, I endured hunger and thirst, and long days in the dark, an uninterrupted night that lasted three months, spent listening out for the faintest sound, trembling with every murmur I heard of the killers above ground, and my only horizon was my hope of seeing you again. The friend who'd hidden me in the basement of the bookstore, a former bookseller who'd retired, was the only person who still knew that this building dated from the Belgian era and continued below the ground; he listened to the rebels' *Muhabura* radio and kept me up to date on your advance. He said, "You'll be liberated soon, your son and his comrades will be here. You'll tell them, won't you, that I protected you?" I agreed and I blessed him. Even if I suspected that he, too, went to man the barricades, even if I had noticed that his gaze had reddened and turned evasive by the end of the month of May. Later I would learn that many Hutus had both hidden people close to them and killed those who were strangers, they were carried away by the imperative of extermination, not to arouse suspicion, because it was hard for them to be brave for longer than a week or a month. I suppose.

You'd been gone for three years, my Bosco. In my putrid

hideaway, while above my head the machetes were decapitating as if on an assembly line, I went over and over my memory of that day in 1991 when the headmaster of the secondary school in Save came looking for you at home. He was a strict man, but fair, and whenever I ran into him in the street in Butare, where he came to buy food for the boys who boarded at his establishment, he would compliment me on your good behavior and your grades at school. When they came into the kitchen of the restaurant to tell me he was asking for me, my heart stopped beating. Were you sick, or hurt, or had you committed some irreparable sin?

My hands began trembling uncontrollably. He seemed preoccupied, but there was no trace of anger on his oblong face. He asked me if you were there. I didn't understand.

"No, he's at school, with you. He left the house along with all the other pupils at the end of the last vacation."

"Bosco left the school four days ago. He showed us a letter, signed by you, saying that your mother had died and you were expecting him for the funeral. We gave him two days' leave but he never came back."

I felt my legs give way beneath me, and just had time to reach for his jacket. He grabbed me before I fell to the floor and helped me to sit on the nearest chair.

"My mother died a long time ago. This can't be."

A burning, diluted blood seemed to be flowing through my body at full speed, sweeping away any attempt my brain might be making to think rationally. What had you done? I kept saying, "This can't be. This can't be."

Your headmaster waited for a long while, grave and silent.

I knew he was a founding member of one of the new opposition parties that began to emerge after the country had been forced to open up to multiparty government. I knew he was a Hutu, but I'd also heard that his mother was a Tutsi, and that he was close to his mother's family, who'd gone into exile in Zaire during the pogroms in 1973.

He cleared his throat, then said, "It would seem Bosco is not the only one who's run away. His friend Ntwali left just after he did, under similar circumstances, a story about a death in the family, and he, too, has disappeared. I suspect they planned this together."

My blood froze, a volcanic mass in fusion that instantly turned cold, and a black stone, a huge jagged rock, invaded all the space in my head.

Before he could have his final say, I had already understood, and the block in my mind was echoing with a single sound, *inkotanyi, inkotanyi, inkotanyi.*

Why hadn't I seen it coming, when you and Ntwali had just spent the last vacation in your room with the door and the curtains closed, listening all day long to the rebels' radio on low? How could I have failed to decrypt your muttered conversations, that look you both had, in the living room, like you were plotting something, lost in passionate discussions with that university student I didn't know? Conversations that turned banal and assumed an air of false detachment whenever I lingered in the room?

So, you were getting ready to join the rebels, the *inkotanyi,* and I didn't realize.

I burst into tears, my hand over my mouth, suddenly feeling sick to my stomach.

The man there across from me must have scrupulously weighed the pros and cons of this explosive piece of news. He saw my distress and adopted the tone of a doctor explaining to a patient who's contracted a highly contagious virus how to keep it from spreading.

"You realize it would be dangerous to let this information get out. No one must know where the children are, otherwise the authorities will harass you. Particularly since you were already imprisoned during the roundup of *ibyitsos* in 1990."

What could I do? Everyone knew everything in this tiny country, where people spent their time spying on their neighbor, where every hill was organized according to an implacable hierarchy: ten families overseen by one person in charge, the *Nyumbakumi*, who would report the slightest incident to the head of the cell, who in turn would relay the information to the head of the sector, who had to file a report to the bourgmestre and so on up, all the way to the prefect and the office of the president, the supreme leader deeply concerned by the growing challenge to his leadership mounted by Rwandans both in and outside the country. How to hide your defection?

My distress must have opened an abyss in my eyes because he lowered his tone even further, as if speaking to a child.

"Don't worry, he won't be the first, or the last. Your son is brave to be lending his support to our exiled brothers who want to come home. The wind has turned and it is driving us irremediably toward change. The greater they are in number, the sooner the oppression of Tutsis and democratic Hutus will cease."

How could he speak like that, like a strategist, envisaging the path to victory, while I saw you dead already, with a bullet in your gut?

"At school, I'll tell them I found both boys seriously ill. To let people think they've got the same disease, that in fact they're doing so poorly that you had them taken to the hospital in Kigali. Save is too close to Butare, we can't have any of their classmates finding out they've been lied to, if they come to visit them here.

"I advise you to leave town for a while, too, to lend credence to this story, and everyone will think you're in Kigali by his side.

"I think it will be easier for you than for Ntwali's parents to make up a story about an evacuation to Europe for health reasons, where you have ties, explaining that his condition has gotten worse. No one must know the truth, do you hear me, no one. Now, collect your wits, and prepare to leave Butare."

He squeezed my hand for a long time with a knowing air and then he left.

Later, I learned that his pupils killed him. They had been prepared to spare him, but he had refused to hand over his mother and his uncles, Tutsis who'd sought refuge with him during the first days of the genocide. I met his widow in Kigali, in early 1997. She had sold their house in Save to go and open a small business at the central market. She was very bitter. I told her this story, told her that you had come home alive and then left again to fight in Zaire. As we were parting, I gave her some money, in memory of her husband's help, and she whispered, "You know, all my brothers are there, in the forests of Zaire, if Bosco comes across them, I hope that he won't make them pay for their crimes during the genocide, but that he'll remember, rather, the good things my husband did." What more could we say to each other now? Our nation had been torn apart; it would take more than a generation to stitch it together again.

Your friend Ntwali sometimes comes to visit me. He always calls me "Mama," and that word hasn't sounded the same to me since your death. When you arrived in Butare, on July 3, 1994, he had a hard look about him, and only ever expressed himself in nervous grunts, or with the few words of Swahili you had learned in the *inkotyani* rebel army. It was him I saw first, once your comrades had taken me out of the bookstore. I was lying on the steps, I could see your boots stirring up the dust in the main road, someone gave me some water to drink. He was standing guard outside the Hôtel Faucon, almost directly across from me, straight as a post, smoking. I felt like going to

ask that young soldier for a cigarette, he vaguely reminded me
of someone. It must've been at least three years since I quit,
but the smell of tobacco evoked a former life that had just been
blown to dust. He called out to another soldier, I trembled
when I heard his voice, Ntwali was alive! At last, I would find
out what had become of you. But he was alone. In my constant
dreams over the last three years, I pictured you both showing
up outside the house, side by side, inseparable since you ran
away from secondary school; you'd be marching or sitting on
an armored vehicle, raising your fingers in a victory sign.
Blanche and I would cheer, the jacarandas in the street would
join in the party, they had covered the tarred surface of the
road with their thousands of purple petals. Your victory turned
out to be quite different. You had conquered a city full of common graves. The flowers fell on abandoned corpses, an
immense silence welcomed you, a cold silence that made its
way into the deepest recesses of your filthy jackets. All that
purple, so many dead. Soon we too, the survivors, would be
covered in purple, the color of mourning in the Christian religion, the first memorial services, churches turned to slaughter-
houses and our shoulders bent to the knife.

Ntwali was alone. Did it mean you were no more? I had to
find out, I didn't dare find out. I hesitated, knowing all the
while that the uncertainty would be lifted at once. What would
have been the point of clinging to hope for a hundred days, of
surviving despite all opposition, if that hope were suddenly to
be crushed?

I lifted my emaciated arm and waved to him, my stiff hand
driving away the air full of apprehension. The sky above Butare
turned darker: was it reflecting the mood of our tormented
souls?

He saw me and crossed the street, walking like a robot.

"Ntwali, do you remember me? I'm Bosco's mother, do you
remember me, my boy?"

He didn't answer right away. His gaze distant, his expression impassive. A grunt. And then, "Your son is here. I'll go get him."

I think I fainted. When I opened my eyes, you were at my side. You lifted me up so very carefully, and carried me like a child, I must not have weighed any more than a child, you took me to a place where other dying people lay.

I only saw Ntwali again when you were leaving for the front in the north, then several months later. In the meantime, you had explained to me why he had become so cold and hardly spoke. The house where he was born had been razed to the ground, and the bodies of his loved ones, which you had found, had been dismembered and half-devoured by dogs; your captain had ordered you to keep advancing, because night was about to fall and you could not risk an ambush before reaching Butare. You told me all that in a tone that was neutral and controlled, you had not been allowed to show any feelings. You were soldiers, exhausted, at the end of your tether, but you had a war to win, a country to conquer. When you were in the bush, and rain and hunger and fear were hounding you, you had thought every day about the good hot meal your mother would make to celebrate your return, and the milk, and the honey, and the beer that would flow over the heroes you were about to become. Ntwali had no one left to wait for him, only blood, flowing, and the swollen bodies drifting down the rivers.

The bitterness of your victory knew no bounds. After you'd taken the entire country, when others were dancing to *Intsinzi bana b'u Rwanda*, "the victory of Rwanda's children," both of you were secretly sobbing and ramming your fist against your throat to stop yourselves from screaming.

Your friend remained a soldier like you, he said, "Where else could I go? What would be the point of studying and working, what would I do with the money I earned if I can't support my parents, and spoil my sisters, and build a beautiful house for my grandmother?" As for you, I begged you to come home, to go back to school. You didn't want to hear it.

And yet it wasn't Ntwali, even though he'd been through so much more, who killed himself. Now he has a wife and children, a reason to work, to stand on his feet.

He was the one who told me how you went to Zaire in 1996 with the aim of finding those who'd killed our families and of bringing them back and dragging them by their feet to the scene of their crimes, and locking them up in deep dark holes where every day they would be forced to listen over and over to a recording of survivors describing the torture they'd inflicted on their neighbors, their friends, their brothers-in-law, sometimes their own wives. With the aim of driving them completely crazy, because killing them would have given them a victimhood they didn't deserve, because killing them would not have brought you relief. You were so naïve, my children, you did not seem to have understood yet that war is not there to bring justice. You were soldiers, not judges, you had a mission, orders to respect.

Ntwali came as soon as he heard you had died. He stayed by my side, no doubt he understood as well as my sister Maria did why I had buried my voice in a place from which it would never emerge. He talked about you, a Bosco I didn't know. Your journey to reach the rebel front in 1991, after you'd run away from the school in Save. The ferryman who rowed you in his pirogue at night across the river Akanyaru, south of Butare, as far as Burundi. The weeks you spent in Bujumbura waiting to be recruited by one of the Rwandan Patriotic Front's secret political cells. That was where you heard that your father had died, dead and buried long ago in his prison in the north. It was the destruction of all your dreams. Ntwali told me you wept like a child, a flood of tears for that man who'd never seen you, who didn't even know you existed, you wept for your country, where agonizing struggles between blood brothers, artificially divided into antagonistic groups, had torn so many families apart—that country you had just banished yourself from, all for a ghost who had vanished a hundred moons ago. When, a few months later, you sent us a short letter that said, "I've gone to be with my father's friends," I understood your motivations for going off to war, Bosco: you'd probably eventually found out that your father'd been held at the high-security penitentiary at Ruhengeri, in the north, with other dignitaries from the south arrested during the 1973 coup d'état. And it was precisely in January, 1991, that the Rwandan Patriotic Army performed a lightning raid on the prison and freed the old political prisoners from 1973 who were held there, Lizinde and Biseruka the most famous among them. You must have thought your father was with them.

How many years did you spend digging for other details I hid from you? As the years went by, you pieced together the puzzle of your origins, the story of your life.

Maybe some pieces were missing; maybe you gave a romantic twist to certain episodes. I know how everything began, and I'm going to tell you. The way a soldier files a report, the way a death certificate is drawn up. It's too late, but I have to do it, for the record, for peace of mind, because it's easier to speak to the dead than to the living. You are in no danger of interrupting me or talking back.

The time for romanticism is over, your heart has stopped, unconsoled, and mine is worn out.

Initially it was your father, Damascène, who loved me, then I fell in love with him. In Save, two secondary school students, an adolescent thing, it could have had a happy end. Except that we were Rwandan, and he was a Hutu, and I was a Tutsi. His family was from Gitarama, I had figured out that you knew this from the way your back would stiffen under my hand in the minibus whenever we came into Ruhango. Your gaze, searching through the crowd at the market: were you trying to find a face that looked like yours, an uncle, a cousin? I didn't ask you any questions, the road led us on to our den of secrecy, our house in Butare.

The Hutus in the south, above all those from Gitarama, held the reins of power in the young, first independent republic led by Grégoire Kayibanda. Widespread discrimination against the Tutsis was presented as a policy of alignment. But in Nyanza, where he was at the boys' school, and I was at the girls', after a few parties which brought us together from time to time, we allowed love to overwhelm us, stupidly, passionately, like every adolescent since time began. Naturally, our parents knew nothing about it.

Your father finished his secondary school one year before I did. He immediately got a scholarship to go and study in Russia at a university in Moscow. My blood ran cold: he would be going to the ends of the earth. The USSR had signed cooperation agreements with Rwanda immediately after our independence, in 1962 or 1963, as it had done with many African countries. Nowadays everyone seems to have forgotten how, during the Cold War, tens of thousands of African students went to get their education in the Soviet bloc—the story of the Patrice Lumumba University, dedicated by Nikita Khrushchev at the beginning of the '60s to the "friendship among peoples." Thousands of young people, from the four corners of the continent, had been able to obtain scholarships thanks to cooperation agreements between states, or thanks to cultural or social organizations, or unions, in order to receive an education in the Soviet Union, East Germany, Czechoslovakia, etc.

Your father was one of them, cleverly juggling between the paradoxical imperatives of the white world, between the Belgians' Christian democracy and the Soviets' radical atheism.

He promised he would tell his family about me before his

departure and marry me as soon as he got back in four years' time. He promised to write to me very often. And he made me promise to wait for him. All those vows. I dried my tears, finished my year without a single letter from him. Time passes more slowly for the one who has stayed behind. Then I got my first job at the Agronomic Institute. Tired of waiting for his letters, I decided to go and knock on his parents' door. No sooner did I introduce myself to his father than he threw me out without further ado. When Damascène came back from Russia, he told me that his family had intercepted all the letters he'd written me. But in the meantime, I'd decided to move on and to find another husband. I'd met Blanche's father, who was a friend of Monsieur Herbillon's, my boss at the Institute. He loved exotic plants and African women. I was lucky, he decided to marry me as soon as I got pregnant. The moment Damascène's family found out, they wasted no time in telling him that I'd erased him from my life, that I'd chosen a white man over him. I hadn't forgotten him, I had just stopped waiting.

The thing was, he came back from Russia professing the same love for me, and pressing me to return it. Blanche's father had to leave the country, but that's another story, not yours.

Damascène wanted to resume our relationship. We shouldn't have. Did I still love him? I don't know, I suppose it was like the first time all over again, he loved me and I fell for him. He took us under his wing, your sister and me—"I'll look after your little Blanche, don't you worry." As if. He would have ended up reproaching me for her existence; she was the daily living proof that I hadn't waited for him like a good girl.

Your father was awarded an important position in the administration of the Republic as soon as he came back from Russia. He became a powerful, influential man. Is it possible to oppose the desire of the powerful, to refuse to live under their protection?

But around the same time, an evil wind began to blow. Once again, like in 1959 and 1963, the Tutsis were attacked verbally, banished from schools, killed. At the same time, Hutus in Burundi fleeing the Micombero regime came here. A group of five Hutu generals from the north of the country seized on the so-called ethnic divisions as a pretext to overthrow President Kayibanda. Your father was arrested, he was in Butare that night, they took me with him. We were separated. I was interrogated. Brutally. It was at the prison that I found out I was pregnant with you. They released me. I would never see Damascène again. Several years went by. I stopped waiting for him, once again. When you began to ask questions, I answered, "He's dead, and that's that."

You didn't believe me. You patiently reconstituted for yourself the puzzle of your origins. When the rebel army freed the political prisoners held in Ruhengeri, you thought your father was among them. You ran away.

That, Bosco, is how everything began. Now I'm the one trying to piece your story together, trying to understand how you came to commit that fatal act. My child, I didn't have you on purpose. All that silence I surrounded you with stifled you. I thought I was protecting you. I lost you.

Ntwali told me how distraught you were, the mistrust they showed you in Bujumbura, how they suspected you of being a spy sent by the extremist Hutu government in Kigali. Illegitimate once again, called on to prove your loyalty. Because your father was a Hutu? Most of them probably didn't know that; I think it was above all because they viewed anyone coming from Rwanda with suspicion, assuming out of hand they'd been contaminated by Hutu Power. Even if your plan to try and find Damascène among the rebels had just disintegrated, you wanted to go on. Were you already looking forward to the bullet that would take you to the kingdom of the dead, where your father's ghost, *umuzimu wa so*, would be waiting for you?

In the end, thanks to a certain need for new recruits for the front, they agreed to let you enlist with the Rwandan Patriotic Army. The official ideology of the *inkotanyi* stipulated that there were no more Hutus or Tutsis or Twa, only one Rwandan people, divided in the past by the colonialists' racialist considerations, and that now they must unite to build a new country. You believed you could take part in this radical transformation of society, and completely change things.

Your friend told me about the long stretches where you marched through the night to go from Burundi to southwest Uganda, crossing huge Tanzania. In silence, poorly equipped, through hostile forests and arid savannas, your hunger and thirst found little sustenance in the milk that Tutsi shepherds from the diaspora sometimes gave you, while they waited for your victory to return to their ancestral lands.

Then the training camp, the hardship, the absolute harshness of life as underground fighters, the fatigue both in your bodies and in your minds, which were being trained, too, in daily sessions of political education. You searched in vain for any of your father's former cellmates, to hear from them what mattered most to you: his last words.

Because your death had plunged me into a deep unspeaking silence, and I couldn't ask your friend any questions, your comrade in misfortune chose what he wanted to tell me, or what he would omit. My gaze was my reply, bathed in tears and gratitude. When, before your death, I had tried to question you about the vicissitudes of your life as a soldier, you had always said that you couldn't talk about it, that you knew nothing about the language in which these things can be shared with a soldier's mother.

Perhaps Ntwali spared me any descriptions of the worst

treatment, the most horrific scenes. He told me you had been incredibly brave, that several times over you had saved his life, particularly when you stopped him from deserting, that there were times you were sent on virtual suicide missions to test your loyalty, and that every time, you came through, miraculously. "It was all those prayers that you and Blanche said for him that protected him."

He didn't want to tell me about the lifeless countryside you went through, or the expeditions you carried out at night, in enclaves still held by the governmental army, in order to rescue the few remaining Tutsis who were still alive, or the time you came upon his childhood home, his family massacred. That is something I learn each year during the commemorative wakes organized all over the country, between April and June, when survivors tell of their ordeal, in public or on the radio. Everyone remembers the day you soldiers arrived—often too late, when there were only a handful left to save. I also attended the trials at the *gacaca* community tribunals on the hill in Ikomoko, to try and find out how my father, my brothers and their families, my uncles and my aunts had been killed, who by and where and in the most horrible way. I didn't find out much, the killers only let out very little of what they knew, in order to receive a reduction in their sentence. All I understood was that their pleas for clemency were purely administrative; I refused to pardon them. And I found out that the scars on my heart were not about to heal.

I accompanied Ntwali, in silence, through all the efforts he made to arrange a burial for his family's remains. I helped him wash the bones and place them in wooden coffins, and build a tomb watched over by a stone where the names of his family members were written, in their memory. We prayed for them; what more could we do?

Ntwali named his eldest son after you, Bosco. He's a sweet boy. He has a large, full mouth and, like you, wide intelligent eyes. He sometimes sends him to me during the summer vacation, I put him in Blanche's room, and I've given him all your childhood books. He doesn't know how to read yet, but he loves looking at the pictures in the comic books. Those books were the only things that weren't looted in 1994, remember?

I recall that, a few days before your suicide, you built a little shelf from the planks that made up the old bench where we used to sit with your sister, for years, on the *barza*. I lost my temper, that object meant so much to me. You answered back, as you pounded the last nail into the tired wood, "The time for children's stories is over, Mama, this will be a little memorial to what we used to be." And on it, you put the relics you'd found in our ransacked house: the books, a rosary, bullet casings, and a bouquet of dried immortelles.

I still don't know what took you from me, my son, but now I know the path that led you there, how our history slowly and surely obliterated you.

Being the carrier of a hereditary genetic disease, when you know nothing about one of your two parents, is a new fear I'm learning to live with. The doctor asked me, "Is there any history of this disease in your family?" For him it was a routine question. I said, "I know nothing about my father's medical history, I never met him." And as if to apologize immediately, to change the subject and mask my ignorance, I added, "But my mother is fine, there's nothing wrong with her." The word *wrong* came back to me in an echo, louder and louder, a parachute going up in flames, a wooden crutch eaten away from inside by an army of termites. I got annoyed: "Never mind the past, tell me how my son is doing, what sort of future he can expect."

Our plans to travel to Rwanda, which we started making three and a half years after Stokely's birth, were now jeopardized. We had to put a lot of things on hold. If we've come here without your grandson, Mama, it's because just before our departure, we found out he has a rare disease that prevents his blood from coagulating normally. The disease is transmitted through the parents, from generation to generation. I'm a carrier, no doubt my father was, too. Maybe I'll find out someday. I thought I knew everything about the sorrow that can be passed on in a family, I had sworn that for my son I would break the vicious circle of our vicissitudes, sweep the path clear for him all around so that he wouldn't collide with the past lurking in ambush at every turn in our lives, the way Bosco and I had. But now with my rotten blood, I've started up again the circuit of invisible woes that binds us, both to life and death. When I called your sister Maria to explain things to her, I could sense her uncontrollable fear. The only blood diseases that were discussed much back in Rwanda were AIDS and hepatitis C. I reassured her that it was nothing like that. Stokely would be getting the appropriate treatment and live as long as if he didn't have the disease, but the hematologists strongly advised against traveling to Rwanda, where they wouldn't have the necessary care. In case of a serious injury, it was vital he receive urgent and regular injections of concentrated doses of the von Willebrand factors, deficient in his blood, to stop the hemorrhaging. This medication, a plasma derivative, was not available in the hospitals in Rwanda; it was difficult to transport, and the child must not be placed at the slightest risk. I don't think she understood everything, other than the fact your grandson would not be coming and you would have to wait a while longer before you could meet him, when we could arrange for you to come and see us. I could imagine how disappointed you were, and Maria could imagine my distress. Added to the guilt of not having noticed the symptoms of my son's disease before he started kindergarten was that of leaving him for the first time without his parents for so long. My mother-in-law, who had worked as a nurse, assured us that everything would be fine, and refused to let us cancel the trip we'd been planning for months.

You came to meet us at the airport with Maria and her eldest grandson, Gaspard, who lives in Kigali now. Wearing your light-colored *imikenyero*, you were like two Roman vestals charged with watching over the family hearth, so often smothered with hatred and despair, although it never went out altogether. On seeing your hands joined under your chin, as if in prayer, I thought of these words from the Catholic liturgy: *O merciful Father, gather to yourself all your children scattered throughout the world.* Not all of them, I've come alone, without my son, and without Bosco, who vanished. But yes, I do feel like a scattered child, a thing dispersed that has come back to where it all began—the fragmentation, the love splattered with secrets, the family in shreds. I'm alone with this husband you once feared would take me to his faraway island and prevent me, with his West Indian heritage, from becoming a true Frenchwoman. My husband who, at the age of twenty, adopted the name of one of the heroes of African independence, without ever having set foot on the continent. He has fantasized for so long about this land, which he calls that of his ancestors, that I already dread he will be disappointed. I informed him that Rwandans—who for so long were protected by the enclosed location of their little country, far from the coast, surrounded by very high hills and defended by a well-organized army—had never been taken captive, never been thrown into slave ships. He didn't care. And all I was doing was repeating what I had heard without being absolutely sure. He said, "It's at the source of the Nile," and I countered, "I think the source of the Nile is actually in Burundi"; he exclaimed with wonder, "What courage, what resilient people," I tried to explain to him the difference between repairing a country and repairing hearts; he wanted to learn a few words of Kinyarwanda, I warned him, "Everyone will make fun of your lousy pronunciation." Why was I painting such a dark portrait of the place we were going? Was I afraid of finding myself projected four years into the past, and my first disastrous return, afraid of finding the hardened, dried remains of our silent meals, the air polluted with Bosco's reproaches and my inability to comprehend his distress, and my too-awkward tactfulness with a mother who was going to pieces? Was I afraid of your silence that had swallowed everything, was I afraid I wouldn't know how to inhabit it, would it seep into my throat and prevent me from saying what I still had to say to you? Afraid, after having been a contingency in your life, of becoming a simple continuity? I was your scattered child.

My husband couldn't understand any of that. How could he? I refrained from sharing my doubts with him, I pretended to be tired from all our preparations and the abrupt interruption caused by organizing Stokely's care, his new medical protocol. We reduced the planned length of our stay from three weeks to ten days, not to leave him too long alone with his other grandmother, who might be overwhelmed in no time.

Another flight with a knot in my throat, no desire to speak, or eat, just the dread of arrival and of facing the land I both cherish and fear, the mother of all my troubles: why wasn't I born in Patagonia?

Four years since I last saw you, my God you've gotten old, Mama! Is it age, or losing your son that has made your hair go so white? On your forehead you're wearing a *urugoli*, that old-fashioned motherhood wreath made of sorghum bark which you probably haven't worn since you married my father. I am moved by this symbol you are wearing for me to see in my very first minutes back on our native soil. You don't speak, but this *urugoli* says a great deal more than any words could, as does the long embrace you give me once we're through customs. When you were young, you used to gently make fun of the way old ladies, your mother and my aunts, would hold us close, shoulder to shoulder, the right-hand side of their brow against the left-hand side of ours, and vice versa, interminably. My brother and I didn't really like these massage-greetings, as we called them, which wrapped us in the smells of tobacco and eucalyptus from their long, faded gowns, greetings they prolonged indefinitely with wishes for herds of lovely *amashyo* cows, to which we could not respond without stammering.

Today I would like your embrace never to end, for all the

illusions, the shame and sorrow to disappear, like a candle flame snuffed between two fingers.

We are unable to part, Maria embraces us in turn with her long thin arms and, when I notice how Samora is hesitating, intimidated and fascinated by our reunion, I take him by the hand and pull him toward our huddled mass. Welcome to our country.

In my nephew's car, as we drive slowly through the night-time capital, languages mix with music. Maria speaks for two in Kinyarwanda, you agree with your eyes, Gaspard translates into French for Samora, our timid laughter is drowned out by the voice of Cécile Kayirebwa singing *Natashye iwacu*, "I've come home"; my gaze gratefully studies the stars twinkling above the hills.

The ten days go by like a series of postcards. My cousins show my husband around the country—the lake at Kibuye then at Gisenyi, the genocide memorial in Gisozi and the one in Murambi, the Akagera National Park, the Nyungwe Forest, the ethnographic museum in Butare, the volcanoes and gorillas of the Virunga Mountains, the genocide memorials at Bisesero and Nyamata, everything running together and blending, I go along with it all, without having the time to think, without having the option of stating my priorities. I would like to have some time alone with you, Mama. I take Samora on a walk through the town of my childhood, he tells me, "I imagined something else, bigger, smarter," I confess bitterly, "I think it used to be, or maybe only in my memory." The French school and Cultural Center no longer exist, nor does the Belgian school, the Arab quarter has lost its market day animation. A few new buildings are going up. The university extension where I used to borrow old books, when the French Cultural Center was closed for the summer, has also disappeared; the university bookstore, where you survived in 1994, has become a hardware store. I wonder where all the books have gone. Most of the university departments have been transferred to Kigali. Buye is a dozy place, Tumba is sullen, Kabutare is no better, Ngoma, too, is half-asleep. These neighborhoods were once my horizons; for so long, I thought that life was here. Yes, we all believed in something during our childhood, both of us, different dreams for each generation. In the end, you and I went further than we would have imagined. But at such a cost. You left your hill, I left my country. And here we are today, our horizons have shrunk, the map is creased, worn, but what remains can always be used to show my son a history, a yarn to be re-woven, the treasure of transmission when it is possible.

Samora has fallen in love with Rwanda, he takes everything in, soaks up the sunshine, the *heart of Africa*, the *incredible* stories. He's told me he wants to write a book. Yet another one. My great-nephews belong to the new generation, they have only a very vague memory of their parents, of the country from before. They have, forcibly, bought into the history being told today. What do they know of nostalgia? For them, it's something you learn by heart at school, without trying to understand, the way, long ago, we used to learn tales and proverbs, and our grandparents' embraces. It looks nice, it gives a certain authenticity to the pride of being a phoenix-country.

Mama, you could be an exhibit in a museum, you know.

The last day has come, the day of all dangers. You have agreed to come to see us soon in France. To meet Stokely. I think that, for him, you might start talking again. The walls of your room are covered with pictures of him. His skin color is the same as mine, we have finally stopped the dilution, and you are satisfied now with café au lait.

We got up early in the morning. The air is very damp, it

would be easy to catch a cold. Your sweaters, your scarves: now you knit all day long, the way your mother did. We dress warmly to go to Bosco's grave. This cemetery is huge, so many dead in the last eight years. You walk ahead, your step firm, I imagine you come here often. I spot it right away, all white, surrounded by colors. The last wisps of mist are lifting above the tombs. You planted fuchsia bougainvillea, and it's blossoming generously behind the cross of varnished wood; on the white tiles, there is a vase with an armful of carnations. You look at me, full of compassion, while I try to pray. All your children scattered, on earth as in the sky, we are here today. A light wind rises from deep in my memory and blows slowly through the cemetery, causing the leaves of reminiscence to quiver, scattering the dust of regrets without further ado. Mama, you have tamed your solitude, as bitter and gray as the smoke from your cigarettes, morning to night; you fight the cold by wrapping yourself in thick woolen armor, vaguely you mull over a past you no longer seek to be free of. You could be an exhibit in a museum, Mama. Now you stay to splatter the roof of your son's final resting place with color. A shower of petals to ward off forgetting. You do your gardening at the cemetery, until you can see your grandson, who has been growing on the far side of the planet, the child who bloomed on the other side of the catastrophe.

On the way home you are reeling, as if you were on the ocean, it's then that I think you've never seen the sea, you've never set foot on a boat, you've almost never left this tiny land-locked country, and I reflect on the expanse of emotions you have nevertheless traversed in sixty years, witness to an era, to the shipwreck of a nation, to the loss of so many illusions. What on earth must you, of all people, think of the resurrection foretold, of reconciliation, of the demons buried just below the surface of the earth, the surface of war? How would you narrate this whole mess if you had the opportunity? Does one write more intensely when speech is gone? Samora would like to write your story, he would like me to tell it to him. I've refused. If one day a novel about you were to see the light of day, only you or I would know how to write it. When every letter is traced with a drop of your own blood, you don't go pointlessly flaunting yourself, you learn to fill the blank spaces with eloquent gazes. It's a question of decency, make of it what you will. People who write about us, those who seek to transcribe our silences, without knowing the score: they sometimes lack good manners. I won't let him transform you into fodder for fiction.

We go back up the road, passing crowds of people. Some stop to say hello, they ask me if I'm here to stay, I say no, but for the first time I come close to contemplating the possibility of moving back here. Maybe I, too, could contribute to this great reconstruction effort. Can you transform an old house without transforming the men and women who've always lived there, who've hidden their hatred in the cracks in the walls, who've planted poisonous seeds at the end of the garden, slipped daggers in the false ceilings?

And if they don't change, where do you put them? In the museum? Countries are renovated like façades nowadays. It makes them look new, until the human means of removing the asbestos and redoing the interior become available. But who will ever have those means? The soul of a nation is a perpetual building site. Spin doctors and media consultants are the new carpenters of a world in storytelling mode. It's a judicious choice, clean and profitable. Is that really what I want? For now, my life is elsewhere.

Your hand is constantly squeezing my arm, as if you were trying to reach me in the hidden recesses I carved out so long ago to protect myself from you, as if to warm them until they melt the cold wax that has invaded everything. You make it clear to me that I have nothing to forgive you for, that none of it was done on purpose, your fingers are soft like a smooth scar, the warmth of a calm heart. Acceptance doesn't mean resignation, is what it seems to say, the smile that comes over your face like the shadow of a dove flying over a courtyard in the late morning sun. Perhaps at last we can get along, without ulterior motives. I probe my heart and acknowledge that the time for bitterness has passed.

Only half a day left to spend with you. You let go of my arm when we enter the forecourt of the house, and with a sweep of your hand, you show me the flowers spilling over from the planters. On the wall a star jasmine, a passion flower, and a white morning glory are climbing, their stems so interlaced that they seem to belong to the same family. So you are not only knitting, you garden all the live-long day, here or at the cemetery. The canna indica flowers that used to be here have been replaced by red hibiscus, and there are still boatlilies everywhere, falling to the ground so now and again it has to be trimmed. On the *barza* in front of the living room you've hung a dozen orchids brought back from the Nyungwe Forest: they adorn the wall with velvet patches, it looks like a fresco of stuffed birds. You've always loved gardening, probably in memory of the two years at the Institute of Agronomic Sciences. You've handed that love on to me, your closeness to plants, hands that are happy to dig in the earth, a nose powdered with pollen. When nostalgia grew too strong, these last years, I would go and walk along the lanes of the botanical gardens looking for *exotic* species. For a year now I've been taking Stokely every Saturday to the new tropical greenhouse in Pessac; he hides behind the mandarin trees or the yuccas, and I say, "Nearly all these plants grow where she lives, your grandmother, your *Nyogokuru*"; he thinks you have a huge park with ten gardeners to maintain it. He doesn't know yet how to tell the grandmother apart from the country, obviously you have created everything that comes from Rwanda. And never mind if these overheated potted plants are the vestiges of colonial plunder, I am particularly fond of flowers that have been uprooted, repotted, exposed, I know that, like them, I am the fruit of a buried past that is still putting down roots.

We go into the living room, you gesture to me to sit and wait, I feel so tired, I'd like to sleep a little, the sofas now have soft green velvet cushions I could lie down on. I would like to sleep for an eternity.

There's a veil of concern in your eyes when you come back and hand me a cardboard box I've never seen. At the last minute, you seem to hesitate about letting go of it, although it's already in my trembling hands. You put your hands on top of it, as if blessing it, then you give a sigh. A beam of light comes in through the half-open door, stains your long motionless fingers with white. The smell of soap rises from the freshly washed cement floor. You sigh and caress my cheek, in anticipation of the tears that will soon flow there, then you turn on your heels, and I can hear your bedroom door close quietly. This is the time for explanations. Will I dare to proceed, now that I feel you and I are at peace?

The box seems old, as if it has come from a distant era I did not inhabit; there is a smell of stale tobacco. I hold it against my belly and carry it ever so cautiously to my room, then sit on the bed and lift the lid.

I recognize my childish handwriting at once, the paper with the little squares of a torn school notebook. The letters I wrote to my father, intact. How did you find them? Maybe after my departure, when the killing began in Butare, you hid initially in the false ceiling? You didn't mention it during my first trip back. I put them to one side, to read them later, or burn them. Did you read them? A first secret unearthed.

I discover other letters, your handwriting, envelopes stamped *Air Mail*, my father's name, the same address I went to in April, 1994, when I arrived in France. They have not been opened. A red stamp, RETURN TO SENDER. The ink almost completely faded. When were they from? I decipher 1973, 1974, 1981, 1991. I'm afraid they might disintegrate if I try to open them, so I put them gently side-by-side on the bedspread.

My handwriting again, the letter I sent you in 1994, to tell you about my arrival in Bordeaux. I went to my father's address, which you'd given me before I fled from Rwanda. A woman, lean, white, opened the door, I asked her if Antoine lived there.

"What do you want from him?"

Suspicious.

"I'm his daughter."

"Come in. You can sit there." Still suspicious, gray, a cutting politeness. "Tell me everything, you say you're his daughter, have you ever met him?"

"No, I just got here. I took out the birth certificate, Embassy of France in Rwanda. Doesn't he live here anymore?"

"Oh, no. That he doesn't."

"Where is he?" Her fingers hardly holding the paper, disdain, as if it had germs; examining me, caution.

"He's dead, Mademoiselle. It's been a while already."

"He's dead?"

"That's what I just said, isn't it?"

"I don't believe you."

"Haha, well, well."

She left me there, then came back with a piece of paper. A

death certificate. A dialogue of documents. Mine, with its smell of exile, against hers, that smelled of mothballs. A disappearance told in administrative formulas—not told, recorded. Artists tell; clerks record, stamp, file, archive. Hearts bury or exhume.

"I figured that if you managed to get away from the fine carnage going on where you come from that you'd show up one morning and ring at my door."

I didn't have the strength to cry. Stiff, motionless on her fine leather sofa, I waited. What for? I don't know.

"And you, who are you?"

"His widow."

"Oh."

"Your mother?"

"She's still there, I don't know if she'll survive. My father's dead?"

"How many times do I have to tell you?"

"Why didn't he ever get in touch, all these years?"

"That, young lady, your mother should have explained to you, she's the one who engineered everything, after all, it's because of her that he had to leave."

"What are you talking about?"

"Oh, I see, she hasn't acknowledged a thing. Fine. After all, someone will have to tell you. She plotted with her lover, your little brother's father, who worked for the government, to have your father deported so she could claim his property."

"That's not true."

"Oh, so what is your version of the facts?"

"I don't have one, but she wouldn't have done that."

"He worked very hard to buy that house and start his restaurant, he always dreamed of making his life in Africa, of living among the Blacks, he loved the Blacks, that he did. We can't say they repaid him in kind."

"Is that what he told you?"

"Yes, of course. He had to start from scratch when he came back here; fortunately, I helped him."

"He never wanted to see me?"

"Only he could answer that, but it's a bit late to find out now."

(Chin up, don't go to pieces.)

"Do you know anyone here?"

"No."

"Well, that was to be expected. I'm not going to put you up, as you can well imagine. But I'll find you a hostel and help you with the formalities, I don't suppose you're going to go home. When you people come here, it's always to stay. I'm not heartless, you know, in France we're civilized, we don't go around killing each other, we take them in, the refugees, the dispossessed. Is that all your luggage?"

"Yes."

You didn't answer this first letter from 1994, Mama, you just said on the phone, "Fortunately that woman helped you a little, I didn't know your father was dead. It's not true what she told you." You gave me no other explanation. So I had to be grateful to my father's widow, and capitulate. That was what you were asking me to do, to resign myself, to accept without protest a legitimate stranger's distortion of your story.

Back then, my feelings toward you vacillated constantly: doubt, hatred, pity, resentment. I had to study, had to get my bearings in the meanders of French life, had to finish grieving for a man I hadn't known, erase that nostalgia for a relationship that had never existed. Move on, and stay on my feet. Chin up, don't go to pieces. Between us was the fact of a genocide that had left you so fragile that it would have been indecent of me to ask you to explain further, to go scraping the recesses of your memory. From now on, nothing would ever seem that important, ever again. To bid farewell to my need for explanations was the least I could do, to show the respect I owed you, when you had just lost your father, and all your brothers, your nephews and nieces, your uncles and aunts.

I broke the seal on the letters Antoine had never read and found your version of the facts. You were completely unaware of everything Damascène had engineered. A powerful man in love is capable of anything. The conspiracy he mounted against the foreign husband, to reclaim his former lover. You'd been caught in the snare of a story that was beyond you. You hoped that Antoine would come back. You didn't mention prison, or Bosco's birth. You didn't ask for forgiveness, you'd done nothing wrong, just tried to get through the events. You claimed you still loved him. A photograph of me as a child, sitting on a bench: Your daughter needs you, she speaks French perfectly. Why don't you answer me? I planted those flowers you love in the courtyard of the house. The regime has changed, come back, everything will be like before. Blanche is ten, she looks just like you. I miss you. A photograph of my confirmation, my immaculate gown, my furtive gaze. Blanche is twenty, she's a woman now, she hopes to meet you someday, she's studying biology at the university, she likes gardening just like you. So it was from him that I got it, and she too must have learned from watching him. Come and see us, at least once. Blanche is twenty-two, the atmosphere here is very tense, I'm worried, would you agree at least to speak to me once? I'm very worried, there's a civil war on, it would be better for her to go and find safety in France. She shouldn't have to pay for what I've done, you gave her life, you owe it to her to protect her.

He never read your letters, Mama. They all came back. Did he ever even hold them in his hands, or did someone else make sure to intercept them first? What is the point now of trying to find an explanation that would put him in the clear?

I'm grateful to you for not involving me in that desperate enterprise, for never asking me to write to him, because then I would have hoped for an answer, I would have gone to the post office every day to see if there was an envelope in our mailbox. I would have come to nothing, a child abandoned to sterile expectancy. During that same era, I was writing letters to him that I didn't send, as if to steel myself against disappointment. Now these two correspondences are united. They, at least, have met.

IMMACULATA

woman discovers a new continent, a child discovers an old woman. The meeting between Immaculata and Stokely was held in a place of non-transmission. People generally say, "At my grandfather's, at my grandmother's, it was this way or that, there were old things, I didn't even know what they were for, or what they were called, we went fishing, she taught me to make the recipes handed down from her mother, we went for walks in places they'd always known, there was a trunk with dusty yellowed books, there were broken necklaces, and chipped earthenware pots she refused to throw out, carefully stored at the back of the shed she used as a kitchen, we went to visit her parents' grave, he introduced me proudly to his companions 'from the old days,' she's the one who taught me about the countryside all around, and told me the story of the centuries-old tree that stood on the crest of the highest hill over there, and taught me what the cardinal points were called, he was the one who carved me my first sling-shot, from the tree he'd planted as a child."

For those two, the knot got tied backwards. It was the grandson who welcomed the old woman into his world and transmitted its codes. "*Nyogokuru*, grandmother, you're going to sleep with me, welcome to my room, to my world, let me show you how the shutters work. Here, in the evening, even if the sky is light the day is over, so you have to close them and sleep in the dark, you mustn't trust the light. Don't be afraid of those loud booms, it's not a war, we call them fireworks, it's

Bastille Day, come to the window and I'll show you. To change the channel, you press here. Give me your hand, you have to be careful not to fall on the escalator. Look! This is called a clarinet, listen, I'll play for you. This is a CD, I'll put on some of the music I like, so you can hear it." He takes her by the hand to show her the places he's always known, his city, his street, his house. She trusts him completely, and yet he always looks out for her approval before he acts. The mother has prepared him, at length: you'll be her guide, but don't ever forget your place: you're a child, you have to listen and obey her. Blanche follows a pace behind, silent, amazed by how easily their relationship flows, as if they've always known each other. It's so obvious. She is the link between the two, but very quickly she withdraws from their conversation, on tip toe, the better to hear them tying their knot, she's like a little garden stake standing humbly in its pot, of little use now, next to the shrub reaching for the sky. A tangible peace has begun to settle over this family, once so broken down, since her last trip to Butare. The time for reconstruction may well have come. Thanks to Stokely, thanks to what Blanche has made of him, putting her life through a sieve in order to pass on only those aspects that are at peace, leaving for therapy her pile of rough stone, anything that has not yet been smoothed or accepted. Blanche has understood she must not confuse everything. Break the cycle of malediction. Not hide, but explain when questions are asked, as close to the truth as a child can understand; avoid letting melancholy take over. And when words failed her, she gave him apertures of poetry. *'Twas brillig, and the slithy toves, Did gyre and gimble in the wabe; All mimsy were the borogoves, And the mome raths outgrabe.* And always the music between them, like a piece of twine tying the stars to their canvas in the firmament, to keep their sensibilities resonating. A constant light they could trust: we know where we come from, that's no reason to drag our feet. We are the black keys and the white keys, the ebony and the ivory, we are the happy proof that rhythm is a question of a heart set free and not of a designated color.

The grandmother arrived exhausted from the long crossing to a country she had once fantasized about. It had taken over three years to finally get a visa. The break in diplomatic relations between the two countries had not helped. Too much rancor, too much pride. The truth about France's responsibility seemed incompatible with its honor. There, too, silence and denial. And in the middle of all the political tension, a few lives on hold, a child waiting impatiently: When is *Nyogokuru* coming to see us? We don't know, but we keep on hoping. She really doesn't talk, really really not at all? No, not at all. How will I know what she wants or how to play with her, then? She's very resourceful, you'll see, you'll manage fine, and besides, you know how to read now, she can write to you. With that in mind, they bought a little whiteboard. He placed it on the bed she would be sleeping in, across from his own.

She sleeps for a long time on the day of her arrival, he stamps his feet outside the door, eager to get her attention. Their first day: what all the time gone by could not contain. He eventually wakes her up by giving her a loud kiss on her forehead. Blanche thinks she looks younger, more alert than three years ago, a smile full of light does not leave her face, and her eyes follow everything Stokely does. They live in a house with a garden now, she motions to her daughter that she wants to sit outside, even though it is a very hot Bordeaux summer. She looks at the flowers her daughter has planted, and writes on the whiteboard with the same fervor as for the first words she wrote on the slate in the school in Ikomoko: "Your bougainvillea is more luxuriant than mine, how do you do it? Will that banana tree give bunches like at home? What's that one called?

It's pretty, do you think I could take a cutting home with me?" She marvels at Stokely's vegetable garden, and he asks her endless questions: "Do you have radishes in Rwanda, *Nyogokuru*? Do you eat them with butter, or dip them in salt? Do you have grapes?" He acts important as he shows her the tools, the fruit, the caterpillars. He jumps from one activity to the next, he can't sit still, he takes out all his games. In the beginning Blanche tries to slow him down: "You know, she's going to be here for three months, you'll have all the time in the world to show them to her." But in his child's head, three months are not enough to make up for all the years without her.

They take her to see the Atlantic Ocean, the endless beaches, the huge waves where young men are surfing, balanced on their boards, like so many commas linking the words of the waves. She dips her feet in, lifting up her skirts, her expression is full of awe, then she spreads her arms as if to freeze the moment, to wrap it up and take it away with her to her little country without a sea. She says to Stokely, "*Yoo*, it's so beautiful," he looks at her, stunned. A hoarse sound, deep but fragile, too, like a chip of brittle black rock, has come from her throat. The stone that was weighing down the lid of her sorrow has been lifted up. He places his hand over his mouth, he is mute with surprise, then turns around, eager to inform his parents, who are walking toward the dunes, she grabs him by the arm, her forefinger to her lips. He smiles, he gets it. She's decided that from now on, only lovely secrets will be kept. The resurrection of words is a revelation her grandson can carry, a miracle within reach of childhood.

Once Blanche has gone back to work, they spend their days just the two of them, harvesting vegetables from the garden and preparing them. He shows her his mother's cookbooks, she learns about spices from the far corners of the planet, they experiment, with some success, she rediscovers the taste of letters as they're pronounced, accents fizzing at the end of her tongue. She makes him start a little notebook of vocabulary from Kinyarwanda to French, he's proud to show it to his parents at the end of every day. An important transmission, stories brought from the other shore, the salt of life in an era of denied visas, the waiting has allowed things to settle, three months to make up for all those years, her words are like unearthed treasure. She hunts through her memory for him, finds the tales of the hare Bakame she used to tell Blanche and Bosco on the little bench on the *barza* in Butare. The pious frogs come back, too, and the songs of the long time of long ago, nostalgia birds.

When he is playing with his video games, during the worst heat of the afternoon, Immaculata sits in the living room, takes a book at random from the bookshelf, and begins reading. Since the catastrophe she's suffered from insomnia, and she'll finish the book when the entire household is already asleep. She's never read so much, devoured so many words, they fill her head with a gentle exhilaration. Sometimes at daybreak she murmurs them in the half-light of her room, and Stokely's faint snoring wraps them in velvet. Birds of the dawn, sounds stolen from the night. At dinner she asks her daughter and son-in-law to tell her about all these Afro-Caribbean writers she found on their bookshelves, and whose stories she has just finished reading. Samora is delighted, he gives her little lectures on Zora Neale Hurston, Chinua Achebe, Bessie Head, *Beloved*, Mariama Bâ, Nadine Gordimer, and *Masters of the Dew*.

Some time has already gone by since Blanche discovered the secret linking her son and her mother, but she acts as if she hadn't noticed. Little wonders must not lose their leaves too soon. The autumn is sweet, she takes Immaculata to visit Paris. A girls' outing, closeness to weave again or rather to invent, for it never has been a part of their lives. Outside Notre Dame the mother forgets she cannot speak and exclaims, "No wonder they colonized us, look what they were building already in the Middle Ages!" Blanche hugs her, to seal the sharing of the secret, and points out with a smile, "If Samora heard you, he wouldn't like it. Nothing justified them colonizing us, Mama, and besides, we built the pyramids long before, didn't we?"

"Yes, you're right, it's good that you two can think like that, I live with my ideas from the past."

"Your era was wonderful, it was a time of pan-Africanism and the great post-independence projects."

"Huh! Look what became of their great projects, look what we've become, I don't know if it was a good idea to dream, you know."

"We mustn't ever stop dreaming. We're the generation who've been writing down your dreams, Stokely's generation might make them happen, who knows?"

"Poor child! What sort of legacy will we leave him? No castles or masterpieces, just trouble and regret."

"But we'll also leave him a history that we've written ourselves, for the very first time, a history of change and pride."

"Don't you go turning him into a revolutionary, will you, the boy has weak blood. Isn't it enough already to have burdened him with the name of a black panther?"

"We won't make too many waves, Mama, stop worrying. The panther is a silent, supple animal when it needs to be."

"Don't forget who you are, or where you come from. Step softly. Know when to stop. If you leap up, you'll frighten them and they'll shoot without warning. Teach him, too, to be a bit of a chameleon."

At the Louvre, she's intimidated: "There aren't too many people like me here," then spends a long time in front of the *Portrait d'une femme noire* by Marie-Guillemine Benoist. Blanche has to admit that the sitter looks uncannily like the young mother Immaculata once was: the same fine nose, full lips, the gaze of a woman who has been silent for too long. The turban around the slave's head reminds her of her mother's wooly hair, now completely white.

They end their city tour at the Musée des Arts d'Afrique et d'Océanie at the Palais de la Porte Dorée.

"But why are there no dates on any of these objects, sweetheart, do they think we have no notion of time?"

"Mama, this all dates from the colonial era, forget it."

She sucked her teeth and said, "And now that the colonies are no more, why don't they send these things back to us, huh?"

"Taking something back is like stealing."

"We never gave them anything."

"Stop it. And anyway, we weren't colonized by France, there's nothing belonging to your ancestors here. The next time you come I'll take you to the Tervuren Museum in Brussels."

"My grandmother always talked about a pipe they stole from her, I could go and ask for it back. And for a start, why do you call them 'my ancestors,' they're your ancestors, too!"

They laugh, the handful of other visitors look at them, failing to understand, surely expecting a more serious attitude on their part, or even sadness, in the presence of *their plundered past*. Blanche savors the moment, this time regained; she is cautious, however, for it is still too fragile to make them forget the rifts, the quagmire of things unsaid. She recalls these words heard at the theater long ago: "You must go on. I can't go on. You must go on. I'll go on. You must say words, as long as there are any—"

Ever since his mother-in-law came to stay with them, Samora has been constantly asking her to tell him, or record everything she went through during the genocide. He has bought her a nice notebook, a black pen with a fine nib, and succinctly explained to her his project for a book: "You give

me all the factual elements, and I'll see to writing it up in literary French and publishing it in both our names."

Blanche doesn't like the idea: "Leave her alone, it's her
story, her private life. And you want to capture her soul, turn
it into a product, adorn yourself with her suffering in order to
shine in company?"

Samora is hurt: "Don't you see how important these testi-
monies are, so the world will know what people like her went
through? It's essential to speak out, to combat all the revision-
ists proliferating in France. I'm not doing this for my own
glory, but for History."

Blanche thinks it's no betrayal of her mother's feelings when
she says, "Do you really think she could tell you only about the
hundred days of genocide, without mentioning what came
before? Old wounds, her fall from grace? Not to mention
afterwards, her son's suicide, the silence she imposed on me,
the lost years, the bitterness? Life isn't made up of neat seg-
ments you can portray separately; her life is a long bolt of
cloth, torn in places, precious, and the story could be rich, but
it's already so threadbare. I don't think your hands are steady
enough for her to entrust you with it. Leave it to those who
have the grit to write their own stories—and I know better
than you how vital they are to humanity. If you want to write
something exotic, why don't you tell your mother's story? She
must have been quite a woman, to raise a mixed-race child
alone in the wilds of the Médoc back in the mid-'70s." The
relationship between the son and his mother has always been
tense; Blanche knows her argument will only hurt him. Samora
falls silent but doesn't give in, and leaves the notebook in plain
sight on the coffee table.

The weeks go by, Immaculata places the books she's read
on top of the empty notebook, then one day, before putting
them back on the shelf, she decides to copy out excerpts.

When the three months of her stay have come to an end, the notebook Samora gave her is filled with an anthology of sentences garnered from the four corners of the Black literary world. She shows it to her son-in-law and says, "Why would you write my tormented story when I can find the polished essence of it in all these writers who've come before you? Reading them has brought me such deep consolation, and I hope you won't hold it against me if I haven't given you anything of myself before going home. It's better this way."

The October days are passing quickly, and the first cold days make her shiver; she's homesick. It's time to say goodbye.

She takes with her a suitcase full of books, seeds, and spices, and promises Stokely she'll write him often. He cries a little, she consoles him briskly: "*Mwana wange*, my child, we only really miss the people we know, I'll come back and see you often. By the grace of God and your mother we are together now."

STOKELY

December 2, 2013

My dear *Nyogokuru*,

Thank you for your letter from February. You know, I think you're the last person on earth who still sends real handwritten letters, snail mail. I really like it. I wait for them impatiently every time (I'm not telling you this to make you think you're not writing me often enough) and it's the first thing I look for when I get home at Maman's on Friday evenings.

I'm getting used to boarding school, I have more friends than at the beginning of the year. I'm in *seconde*, it's like the fourth year of secondary school for you. You see, I know a lot of things about the time when you were my age in Rwanda. With the internet I can spend hours reading about your history. On the weekend when I'm with Maman I ask her questions, and she thinks it's very funny. She regrets not teaching me Kinyarwanda, but I have to confess I don't really miss it that much. It's a pity I can't come and see you in Butare.

The photo album you sent me is great. I know you didn't do it on purpose, but the negative got double exposed somehow, and it made these really cool images. On every photo there's a place behind a place—your house is floating on the lake water, the birds have their wings spread on your eucalyptus bookshelf, the red sardine cans are balanced on the highest branch of the silk-cotton tree in the middle of the cotton buds, it looks like Christmas decorations on a snowy fir tree. It's as if everything was about to vanish or be covered in a ghostly mist. Yes, *Nyogokuru*, your album is full of ghosts, and that's what I like about it. I wanted you to tell me about your world, with photographs, just the places, the objects, and the animals, and it's as if all the people who are gone, the dead you keep inside you, have come to say hello to me. I enlarged the photographs and tacked them on my bedroom walls. When I'm in bed I can go into one of the scenes and make up an adventure where you and Maman are the heroines. I imagine other lives for you, stories that always have a happy ending. *Sinjye wahera hahera umugani!* I asked Maman what it meant, that phrase you always said at the end of the stories you used to tell me when I was little. "Let it not be the end of me but the end of the story!" That's really beautiful. Storytellers never really die, isn't that right? I think I'd like to be one, later on, you know, a storyteller, to kill the time that murders the people we love, to keep a trace of the commas between yesterday and today. Maman explained to me, too, that in Kinyarwanda you use the same word to mean yesterday and tomorrow, *ejo*. That's impressive. In history class I made a little sculpture with a long piece of wire I found in the courtyard: I made ten "ejo" attached to each other, "ejoejoejoejoejo," and then with this metal sentence I made a ball the size of a fist. Like a globe. I'll put an iron stalk on it and give it to Maman so she can plant it in the earth next to the hibiscus I bought her for her birthday, and which is still blooming.

Ejo, yesterday and tomorrow, it's your time and my time, joined in the same word. You see, we're always together.

I have to go to the cafeteria, *Nyogokuru*. I'll mail this

letter tomorrow. It's supposed to snow tonight, maybe I can put a snowflake in the envelope.

Lots of hugs and kisses, *Ndagukunda*.

S.

April 20, 2014

My beloved *Nyogokuru*,

How are things in Butare? I know you're dreading the great rainy season, and the cold weather that makes you cough all the time. And then, I know, too, yes, that April is here again . . .

Spring is slowly coming.

Maman is leaving tomorrow on her second mission to Mozambique for Doctors Without Borders. She'll be gone for three months. On weekends I'll go to Papa's place. We're getting along better, I don't know if I told you in my previous letter. The talk we had helped me a little to accept certain things. It's their life, and I mustn't take sides. And they did everything possible not to tear each other apart in front of me. In the beginning I was angry with them for sending me to boarding school, but I've realized it protected me from the smell of spite that filled every room in the house. When I talk to friends whose parents are divorced, too, they tell me things that are really just too awful. At least we've stayed on our feet. For a long time, I thought that because of your family history—her father, the genocide, Bosco's death and all that—Maman was the most fragile member of the family, and that Papa was protecting her from herself and her "Rwandan demons." Now

I know that if there was anyone who did what had to be done to rebuild their life, it was Maman. She's not unsinkable, but she'll stay the course. As for Papa, he's always taken refuge behind his chosen identity, but it's like a suit made of paper that the first rainfall could wash away. He's given up looking for his father, and he never stopped arguing with his mother. And when she died, it was as if a dike burst inside him and flooded the village where he grew up. It's not easy for me to see my father looking lost, incapable of clinging to roots that are deeply buried somewhere. I've held it against him. Papa is missing the kind of place that would let him say "us." He wears his skin like a banner and unfurls it at the slightest provocation. But if you lifted a corner of it, I don't think you'd find either flesh or bones underneath, but a terrifying white emptiness. Now I see that he's jumped on the bandwagon of politicians who want to display a man of color on their campaign photos, he's become the spokesman for the memory of slavery in a city that has hidden its slave-owning past for so long; sometimes he even uses your story—"My son's grandmother is a survivor of the genocide"—to increase the weight of his suffering. Papa seems small to me. He has a real problem with legitimacy.

And yet, it's important to fight. Racism is still present, even for me, every day, in the most imperceptible things. Last week in the cafeteria, when I refused the avocado on my plate because it was going black, the cafeteria lady said, "Why don't you go back where you came from, and see if they aren't all black back there!" And I didn't say anything. Yesterday, the girls in my class spent all of recess putting their hands in my Afro and saying, "It's so soft, it's like lambswool, or angora!" There's one other mixed-race kid at the lycée, his name is Ruben. They can never tell the two of us apart. He's small, with a flat nose and long smooth hair like an Indian's, just the opposite from me, but our skin, our skin—that's all anyone sees. It doesn't make me angry, and if I didn't have the parents I have, I would have thought it was normal, but now I notice everything, and every time it's like a splinter inside me, a tiny cut invisible to the eyes of the world. It's like what my disease would do when there's internal bleeding if I didn't take my coagulants.

I know that twenty years ago it was even more complicated for Papa, I can imagine what he went through, and that can explain his anger. Was it the same for Maman in Butare? She often says, when I come out with Papa's antiracist slogans, "I'm not the one to talk, when you see what happened where I come from, when Hutus and Tutsis were the same color, spoke the same language, had the same religion . . . Who was I to go telling whites how to behave?" And then we get into one of those long discussions about the history of Rwanda, like this: I say, "It was the white colonialists who rammed their nineteenth-century racist theories onto traditional Rwandan society, changing social categories that were actually more tenuous and shifting into ethnic groups, spouting theories they were quite happy to reproduce, without thinking them through, without making an effort to understand, because for them, after all, you were no more than poor Blacks."

And Maman answers: "But why did we go along with that? It wasn't white hands that were holding the machetes, as far as I know! And why so much cruelty? The authorities had said, 'We have to eradicate,' they could have simply done a clean job of beheading people with a single blow, like executioners in the Middle Ages, why so much sophistication and inventiveness in horror—clubs studded with nails, shards of glass shoved up women's vaginas—well?"

And me: "But do you really think they would have killed

one million people in three months if they hadn't had the support of the French president and his government, if the United Nations hadn't withdrawn the peacekeepers right at the beginning of the massacres?"

I remember what you said to Maman one day: "He's still a child, stop bothering him with all that trouble." All that trouble, I'm the one who went looking for it, *Nyogokuru*, reading my mother's books when she was at work, secretly watching documentaries on YouTube, the kind she would have thought were too violent, for sure. Whether you like it or not, that trouble is mine, too. I've made room for it in my life, without appropriating it the way Papa wanted to. I decided to immerse myself in it, my eyes wide open.

Today an old Jewish man came to speak to us at the lycée about his experience. They gathered us all in the cafeteria to listen to him. As a child during the Holocaust, he'd been hidden. He told us how his parents had sent him to the south of France then to Switzerland, the yellow stars they'd had to sew onto their clothes, the fear and hunger. His father and mother were deported, they never came back from the camps, he was raised by his grandmother, who survived. It was very moving. I felt ashamed and annoyed to see that the other students were distracted and weren't really listening. I was upset, even though I've already seen a lot of films about the Holocaust. When he'd finished speaking, I went up to speak to him. I told him that my grandmother had survived another genocide and that today was April 20, a sad anniversary, that it was twenty years ago to the day that the massacres had begun in her city, Butare. I don't know if it was because he was tired, or his hearing aid wasn't working very well, but he didn't seem to hear me or to be listening to me. He just said, "Oh, yes, Roo-anda, the Hutus and the Tutsis, that was awful, yes, Africa is tough, isn't it, even today, just look at all those people fleeing to Europe." And then he left. I was really disappointed, I didn't even ask to take a photo with him, even though I'd wanted to, to send it to you with this book I've just finished, one Maman gave me. It's by Imre Kertész, he was about my age during the Holocaust, and his sarcastic tone reminds me of you. You'll write and tell me what you think of it?

Many kisses across the sea and the hills, my *Nyogokuru*. I hope the days are treating you well and that you've managed to catch your breath. So many thoughts for you today, April 20.

Stkl

July 5, 2016

My beloved *Nyogokuru*,

I'm giving this letter to Maman, since she'll be coming to see you tomorrow. It's been so long since she went to Butare, I think she's a little nervous. You'll talk to her, won't you? She needs for you to comfort her, she broke up with her boyfriend. Maybe you can convince her to give him a second chance. It's complicated, because they live far apart, he's in Lisbon and she's here, so one weekend a month is not enough.

Anyway, I'm sticking my nose into something that's not my business, you'll see whether you want to speak to her about it or not. It's ironic that it's a real Mozambican who replaced Papa in her heart, when he took for his pseudonym the name of the great liberator of that country, a place he's never even been to. Like her, he goes there on regular missions for Doctors Without Borders. He's the one who gave me the book I'm sending to you, *The Land at the End of the World*. Maybe you'll think that Antonio Lobo Antunes's language is a bit raw. But I was thrilled by his desperate poetry. It's the honest gaze of a colonialist on the wars of independence.

A few times in recent months I went with Maman to meetings or commemorations organized by the community. I don't know if she told you, but for a while now she's been fairly involved in associations for the commemoration but also other things, sometimes in Paris. I realized that I was beginning to feel left out, not speaking more than a few words of Kinyarwanda. I bought an old textbook on the Internet and I'm going to get started this summer.

Now that my baccalaureate exams are behind me, I'll have more time. I'm waiting for my results but don't worry, it went fairly well.

I'm very happy, too, to be sending you my first published text. It's my short story, "The Severed Country," which won the prize of the Lycéens' Competition last month. So now I have the feeling that it's here, within reach: I can tell stories, draw commas between the hinter-world and the here-on-earth.

Sinjye wahera hahera umugani!

Stokely

PS1: I had a good laugh when they handed out the prizes. The president of the jury, an old linguist who apparently is very well known, who had asked me before I went up on stage where I was from (obviously he didn't ask the two other winners the same question, because they were white), anyway he didn't stop saying that he'd been very moved by my story set between France and Zaire. He mixed up the two countries, and not only that, he used the old name for the DRC, which no one's been using for nearly twenty years!

Lots of kisses, my *Nyogokuru*.

PS2: The story is a mixture of fiction and reality, you'll see, even if I was inspired a little by our own lives, there are differences, and I hope you'll understand and won't get angry that the grandmother in the story was killed in 1994 . . . fortunately for us you stayed alive.

Kanuma, your little storytelling dove.

The Severed Country

This is the story of a couple who are drowning. Long ago, in the first days, before they began taking on water, they had conversations about tenderness, they had plans crackling with excitement like crickets at the heart of a sunny day. They had met in the rain, brother and sister at arms in a heroic struggle of that era, against discrimination, injustice, and climate disaster.

They recognized each other, on the right side of conscience.

They advanced in unison, tall and proud, as if for a military march.

Love, when it is still fresh, is alluring, full of slogans.

After the parade, the engagement, the dowry, people's speeches, the wedding cake, other people's speeches, the wedding rings, the fireworks, there come the Sundays of ordinary time. A child is on the way, plans become reality. Until now they had gone from one island to the next, nothing mattered provided they were together every night, under the sea, where the islands embrace in secret. But when you grow up, you return to the mainland. Mine, yours? She said to him, "You're my country." As if wisdom were already moderating their ardor, they chose safety. His country it would be. Old, solid, reassuring. It was in the north, the cherry trees were in blossom.

In the middle of winter, a son was born. There could also have been a dog or a cat for him to play with, it was something you often saw in that land. But by the time the idea came to the father, who had grown up there, or even to the child, she had already gone into exile in her thoughts, far from them, and she replied, "That sort of closeness with animals, that's not something we do where I come from."

"Where you come from? And where am I from?" asked the son, even though he was her spitting image. Angels passing, wingless, overhead. The mother hesitated. Already? Only yesterday her boy had been merely an idea against the background of July's throbbing music, and now he was asking sharp questions, dropping hard pebbles in her shoes, though she had taken the care to polish them well. Wings flew over, eager to find their mistress. The father's silence, waiting for an answer, an indication, like a nod, what to think.

"You are mine and, consequently, in addition, you are also a little bit from there, but today you are, first and foremost, here, which explains why you have strange urges, like allowing an animal to take a place in your life and on your bed."

The father observed him with a smile. For a long time, he'd been anticipating this moment, when their child would at last break through the armor in which she had slowly been enclosing herself ever since they set up household in this middle kingdom on the coast of opulence. When he had begun asking questions about her before-time. You don't ask a lover to tell you about the errors of her ways, but once she had become the mother of his child, he realized she had told him nothing about her early years. He questioned her relentlessly, until he understood that she had shown him only a post card in faded colors, a dog-eared family photograph, a jacaranda flower embroidered on the handkerchief she always carried deep in her handbag. In daytime, she reassured him, everything was fine, she was all serenity, but the night-time was gashed now with the baby's crying, and in the hollows of her new sleeplessness he came upon unmistakable terror, tears of madness.

The accumulated fatigue revealed what was going on underneath. And so, because he still loved her, he thought he would manage to root out whatever it was that was haunting her repeated nightmares, the way you remove a rotten tooth from a mouth clenched shut in pain.

At least speak to him in your language, you don't sing him any songs, I never hear you uttering those consonants that link you to the childhood you escaped from. Incomprehension, how can I explain, it's not that I've forgotten the lullabies, but you know they say that the neck is the lid of sorrow, and the lullabies are still stuck in there, to get them out I think I'd have to slit my throat.

Don't say that.

There's always something left, even when everything has been destroyed. It is silence that devastates those who remain, that walls up the void you stop yourself from telling him about. Silence kills memories.

I can't sing anything for him, everything inside is torn to pieces, I think I've succeeded in shutting myself up not to let anything get out, because what I contain is in danger of hurting you both.

I remember a proverb that said we can escape from whatever is running behind us, but not from what is running inside us.

Then teach him to listen.

She turned down all the books he bought, which he had dissected in search of clues to understand her invisible scars, the ones she had camouflaged. He went looking for record albums, took out old cassettes she had buried, and forced his son, once a week, to watch his mother, her lips mute, gesticulating to the rhythm of melodies with broken words. The little boy grew bolder: "What's this song about, mommy?"

Sometimes she took a few dance steps, the story of a broken calabash, of an Intore with a mane of sisal, and as the years went by, she agreed to share her debris with him, old melodies, tears flowing inside, everything a young woman had once tucked under her arm as, gasping for breath, she ran away from hatred and the cleansing of her loved ones. She yielded to him when it came to music and dance, but not words. He said, "Please, give him the key to enter, how can he ever get in without knocking on your door so that it will become his home, too?" Words, even foreign ones, even ramshackle, patched-up ones, can re-create, evoke what was. But when tongues have been severed by the teeth that were supposed to protect them, when fathers and mothers have turned away from the fruit of their loins, a grave-digging silence wins. There were times she shut herself off, leaving them on the threshold to her story, especially in the springtime when the flowering trees prevented her from breathing. She said, "These are not stories for children, these are not tales for the living, I want my son to be on this side of what exists, I don't want the flowers to make him sneeze, he'll be stronger without a reaction, he'll walk straighter without a fragile heel."

This is the story of a family that is drowning.

Then one day, a strange woman came from there and brought with her a photograph, and everything simply collapsed. The image of a woman with long frizzy hair piled high on her head, apparently intimidated, arms crossed, her hand hiding a smile, her eyes amused. In the distant background behind her you could just make out a jacaranda tree in black and white. She told them about this magical tree that poured purple rain on her child's feet. She made a little altar in the middle of the living room, at the heart of the house, on the tossing island. She brought them together, as if for a lesson, and murmured, "Forgive me, now I have to scratch the surface of things." She said a name that sounded pretty, "Immaculata. That's where we come from, she was my continent, my country, my reason. Now I will speak to you." The silence cracked, letting a new horizon appear, still uncertain, the smallest of waves could have erased it, they slipped their moorings, ready to go there, but aware that the least little thing could cause them to capsize.

And so, one morning at dawn, they fly away, the woman and the jacaranda wrapped in a handkerchief deep inside the mother's wallet, just next to her heart beating fit to burst. And the hours they spend together, listening to the surviving melodies, carry this beating in their mixed blood, their hands held, the unmoored island floats then lands in unison. The child looks at a woman who is learning how to walk again, to eat, to speak. She had lost the binding properties of language, she says, "I lost the words, the nuances," she mispronounces, stumbles, starts over, apologizes, gets lost in explanations with strangers, I left a long time ago, why didn't you come back sooner, systematically the sidelong reproach quickly swept away by her enthusiasm, no I'm here and I'll come back so often that I'll stop stumbling like a foreigner in our language. Familiar sounds lurk behind every reflection of the light; objects, dust, the gazes of her kind which tell her you are one of us, and delighted she takes her son and pushes him ahead of her, points to him and says, "He's mine, and through a ripple effect, he's yours, too." The gazes of her long-lost brothers and sisters are not saying no, face to face, they flee in search of the wave edges on the water, where the ripple effect ends with their blanched skin. These are the instants when the island is reshaped, and the herd recalls the danger of sinking straight down because everything is still so fragile, and the mother understands that here, too, her striped child will have to justify, to prove, to be forgiven for always being different.

And so, to console him for this exile which, she has warned him, will be constantly renewed, she gives him treasures for the palate, for that is something she has not lost, not at all, the first taste, the sugar, the spice. It's a season of juicy, fragrant fruit, she teaches him how to pick, peel, season. At the market she hurries from one stall to the next, enchanted to see it all again, to pass on the knowledge of appetite and mouth-watering smells. She teaches him about fingers that knead, about cassava, a paste for shaping and scooping up the peanut sauce with little fish from the lake, green eggplants, bitterness swept away by the fiery bird pimento, the sweet potato that melts in your mouth, grilled bananas, braised goat; the best skewers are at the turn in the road just before you head down to the capital, the queen of avocados can be found at the nuns' in the South, before the great ambush of the bamboo plantation. She tells him, taste that, there's nothing better on earth, and he believes her. The passion fruit, only just ripened and picked straight from the vine for stolen kisses, green mandarins with their perfume of vetiver against the erosion of hearts, she teaches him to part the twinned little bananas behind his back so as to ward off the fate that would make his offspring greedy. Is it bad to be greedy, mommy? Yes, but they love chubby children here too, so go ahead, drink some junket, drink, drink, and then we'll go and greet the cows, the flocks, the grass is growing again on the burned earth, and there where she thought it had been cut down, a cauterized branch is growing, vigorously, with a thousand smaller branches, a forgotten then found repository of feelings, which the silence had nearly submerged for good.

And sometimes when the mother falters on seeing a still-fresh cut on a path overgrown with brushwood—where, in the old days, she'd been all siblings' plans, laughter mixed together—when she says, "Friendship was a path we maintained with our feet, there's no one here anymore to pull up the weeds, the last footprints were blown away ten moons ago by an evil wind," the son finds the gestures to carry her, console her, keep her from collapsing.

Then it's time to go home, unless it's a new departure. The vacation is over.

And the father? He carried the bags, the souvenirs from the market, he took photographs, recorded the magic of puzzles pieced together before their eyes, in their veins. He recorded a thousand flowering jacarandas as his film unrolled. He feels the satisfaction of the seamstress who finishes her work before daybreak and falls asleep thinking, "My children will be wrapped up nice and warm to get through the winter." He's cold, he's already shivering at the thought of the emptiness she'll soon leave him with, he's seen it in her eyes, on the tarmac: she promised the uncoupled sun, "I'll come back, when it's jacaranda season again, I'll bring my life here, from back there." The father knows he will not follow her, because he knows he has prepared the warp, has stepped away bittersweet from his loom. He has seen the Africa he dreamt of and has understood that he is irreparably foreign, in spite of his ancestors, in spite of his chanted *négritude*. Here, what would there be to fight for? No bitterness, however; he can rest assured that his mixed-race son, at least, has found the keys, and will know how to maintain the restored pathways with their traveling feet.

It's the story of a couple that made a long crossing.

When love grows weary, you mustn't insist.

For them, in the end, the story finished well, they avoided sinking and they learned that in the severed country, islands can become hills that meet in the valley, behind a bookstore.

THE JACARANDAS

One morning in November, a few months after her daughter's last visit to Butare, Immaculata dies.

What did mother and daughter say during their last moments together? It doesn't really matter. They had been speaking for a long time, their tone of voice was gentle, like well-curdled milk, their gazes did not flare or wither. The time from long ago had been de-mined, they both knew how much the other had tried, in her way, to do her best, without forcing it to be perfect.

As a legacy, Immaculata wrote an enigmatic poem to Stokely, where she invited him to follow the path of black felt-tip ink she left on the white pages of her bookshelf. *"My little comma storyteller, all these books tell better than I ever could of the bitter-sweet smell of eternity. And if one day you feel alone, because we're all gone, you'll be able to find a certain kinship preserved here among them. Between words and the dead, there is only a breath, all you have to do is capture it with your lips and be sure every day to make up a bouquet of remembrance."*

Blanche is winding up a mission in Zimbabwe when they call with the news. By the time she manages to get a flight through Johannesburg, four days have gone by. At the airport, when she sees her son next to her aunt Maria, waiting for her, she feels her legs might give way.

"I couldn't not be here, Maman, don't be angry with me. Don't be afraid, I took out first-class repatriation insurance in case there's a problem, and I have all the medication I need. I'm here to pay tribute to a life, not to spoil my own. From now on I'll decide for myself which dangers I can assume; my imperfect blood won't stop me from being where my heart tells me to go."

They lay Immaculata to rest next to Bosco, beneath the tall fuchsia bougainvillea she'd planted. Their graves will be protected from the sun by its abundant foliage, and from monotony by its colorful petals.

Stokely has brought his clarinet and plays a melody for her, as poignant as a Kaddish.

It is when they return from the cemetery that Blanche realizes the two jacaranda trees that were on either side of the house for as long as she can remember have been chopped down. And she who has kept her calm throughout, consoling others and organizing things without ever faltering, suddenly breaks down. Those trees symbolized something fundamental, who they once were, the three of them, Immaculata, Bosco, and her. They were impassive witnesses, the silent accomplices of all those years, before and after the family was reduced to shreds, witnesses to the slow act of mending she had undertaken by coming here from time to time, with caution and stubbornness.

Why are they gone?

Maria tells her they caught a blight and dried up very quickly, that there was nothing to be done, they died shortly before her mother did. For a long time, Blanche cannot move from there, goes on sitting on the trunk of one of the dead trees, her back to the house, her gaze lost in the reflecting windows of the bland, newly renovated façade of the Hôtel Ibis across the way. Maybe it is then, submerged by a melancholy that rises in her throat like an uncontrollable shudder, like an old childhood splinter gently removed from a wrinkled hand, that she makes her decision.

For her plan to be implemented at last, it will take the negotiation of a breach of contract from the hospital; several trips and long conversations with her lover to persuade him to come and spend the winter months by her side, from December until the jacarandas are in flower in Lisbon; and above all, the news that she is the sole heir to her father's property, once his second wife has died.

On the main street in Butare, after a long time has gone by, in the place where Immaculata and Maria once served up plantain stew and spicy goat skewers, Blanche opens a library. Twenty-five years after the closing of the bookstore where her mother had survived, hidden in an unsuspected cellar, it was a mad venture. On its modest shelves were the books that Immaculata had loved, in French and English, and which, she hopes, will be translated into the local language as well in her lifetime. There are books in Kinyarwanda on history and culture, written by Kagame, Bigirumwami, or Muzungu. And in the display window, like a talisman, is the book she likes best of all, the first novel from Butare, *My Trances at the Age of Thirty*, written by Saverio Nayigiziki in 1949, the year she was born. There are a few odd chairs, one or two secondhand tables, tea is offered in chipped cups, and memory here has the scent of old paper. Blanche has turned the former kitchens into an audio room, and all day long, visitors can sit in a big armchair made from woven banana leaves and listen to actors reading stories on her stereo, on records come from far away. On Saturdays it is Blanche who brings the stories for children to life. When there are power outages, they come there, suddenly at a loss without their television, and in their wide-open ears the echoes of immortal things resonate: *cyera habayeho, il était une fois,* once upon a time.

Stokely comes to join her for the summer. She knows she can't stop him, and bends to his will by surrounding him with multiple precautions. Time passes slowly in this city from the past. Sometimes, when it rains, young people take shelter in the house of books she has named, "Blue Flamboyant," in memory of the vanished jacaranda trees.

He shows her the branches that have sprouted from the trunks in front of the house, already forming imposing bushes where once there were only tree trunks: "You're letting the shoots grow? Apparently it's pointless, they'll never produce either flowers or fruit. Why don't you uproot them so you can plant new trees? Eucalyptus, for example, they grow quickly, and they smell good."

But Blanche refuses. She knows how political trees are. The jacaranda, whose magnificent lavender blue blossoms are the pride of Pretoria, Nairobi, and Bulawayo, is not an African plant. It is native to South America. The colonizers imported it and planted it all through the lands of their vast empires. It is a species with invasive roots that prevent any life nearby; it requires a great deal of water and sucks the soil dry. It has become a symbol of the colonial past. Just like the eucalyptus, which is native to Australia, it was used by the colonizers to drain the swampy regions in the hopes of combating malaria. The whites left, but their trees stayed, plant relics of a history that has not stopped producing shoots.

"No, I'm not going to uproot those trunks, Stokely, and I don't see what it would change, replacing them with eucalyptus trees. Maybe I see something of myself in those shoots. If I'd been uprooted, you wouldn't be here today, nor would this house where young people like you can come and take in the words of Fanon, Diop, and Ngũgĩ Wa Thiong'o."

At the end of the day, when a cool little wind gently covers the tiled and corrugated iron roofs of Butare, the son and the mother find themselves sitting on the *barza* in the main street.

At the craft cooperative, Blanche found a very old bench made of an unknown wood: the tradesman was reluctant to sell it to her. He couldn't understand why she preferred precisely that one, which was completely worn, he wanted her to pick from one of the sturdier ones, or a brand-new one, which in his opinion were more desirable. Blanche is saddened by how her kind are so irresistibly drawn to everything new and modern. She is so attached to what has vanished, and would have liked to tell the tradesman how precious old objects and houses are, how they are treasures of potential remembrance within the heart's reach, helping to bear the absence of all those who are no more.

But she merely paid for the bench and hurried home to show it proudly to her son, as she said, "You and I, thanks to this old thing, will be able to revive an ancient family tradition."

She told him about the evenings in her childhood when Immaculata would prepare them for bed by telling them the myriad fantasies of the land of a thousand hills, the treachery of Bakame, or the brave deeds of the royal dynasties, which she interlaced with a few verses from the poetess Nyirarumaga. She told him that it was on this bench that she understood the beauty of her mother tongue and the power of words, when you dare to set them free from their cocoon.

Over the last few months, to prepare for his second stay in the country, Stokely re-immersed himself in his Kinyarwanda textbook. Now he has asked his only Francophone cousin, Arsène, who made the incongruous choice for the time to stay in Butare and study literature at the University in Ruhande, to give him a few lessons. Every day at the end of the afternoon, they work together at the table in the living room for an hour, studying vocabulary and pronunciation. The grammar, which is too complicated, will come later. Stokely plans to spend three months here. One evening, not long after the bench arrived on the *barza*, he asks his mother if he can add something new to their tradition: a little battery-operated cassette player, so they can listen quietly on the terrace to the cassette his grandmother sent with her last letter to him, containing the melody composed before the war by the great poet Cyprien Rugamba, and sung by his choir, the *Amasimbi n'Amakombe*. Stokely is determined to learn it by heart, phonetically, while he works on mastering the language. The song is called "*Akabyino ka nyogokuru.*" Blanche translates the lyrics for him.

> *Grandmother's little dance,*
> *She got old and left me here on earth*
> *I'll make this dance her memorial*
> *I'll gather everyone my age*
> *so they'll join with me in singing*
> *I'll teach them what to respect*
> *This woman with her crown of motherhood*
> *must not see her name forgotten*
> *We her children must dance for her*
> *I'll dance to wear the aura of her memory.*

Blanche shares memories from her mother's childhood with him—the elementary school in Ikomoko, where they'd memorized songs in French that she wouldn't understand until several years later.

She tells him how glad she is to see him growing attached to her native language, and she apologizes again for not managing to teach it to him when he was little. "You'll see, Kinyarwanda is full of recesses, hiding places, it's a bit devious, you know, like we are." She reveals the fact that her name, *Uwicyeza*, has a double meaning. *Icyeza* can have two roots. The first is: *ikintu cyiza cyane*, a very beautiful thing, *Uwicyeza* is a woman graced with a thousand beauties. But the second meaning refers to an ancient Rwandan mourning rite. When people went into mourning, they covered themselves with ash. That was why, for example, the authorities decided to replace the purple color of the Christian rite with ash gray during the commemorations of the genocide, no doubt for greater *authenticity*. When it was time to celebrate publicly the end of the mourning period, the ash was removed and replaced with white chalk. The person officiating during this whitening ceremony was called *Icyeza* or *Uwicyeza*. For a very long time, she'd only known the first meaning of her name; it was only very recently that her aunt Maria revealed the second meaning, during a conversation about the family. Maria also told her that her grandmother Anastasia had been something of a medium. It was a secret she alone knew, and her mother had made her swear never to reveal it to anyone, neither her brothers, nor her sister, nor even their father. Maria explained that Anastasia, in a dream, had seen something of the misfortune that would strike Immaculata. She had hoped that in giving Blanche that particular name she would be the one to lift the sorrow from her mother's heart and set her free. Blanche sighs, "My grandmother was wrong." Stokely protests, assures her that in the end she succeeded in banishing the silence and resentment from their lives, and in weaving a knot between the generations. With almost no accent he says, "*Uwicyeza, uri umubyeyi mwiza.*" You are a good mother.

A flight of bats carries their clear, mingling voices to the end of Butare's main street, and perhaps even beyond, as far as the ruins of Ikomoko. Night is about to fall.

Blanche places her hand on her son's shoulder. She motions to him to wait before pressing the button on the cassette player.

In the fresh air of the spent day, at the very moment when

a blood-red sun is disappearing behind the crest of the horizon, she entrusts him with the most precious thing she knows.

"We are Immaculata's descendants, the children of the twilight of Butare. In France they call this twilight moment the hour between dog and wolf because you can no longer tell the two canids apart. Maybe we should call it, rather, the hour of mixed races. We are the stream of crystal-clear nuances that flows between monotonous walls, a trace surviving amid shouts, or hatred and love, one or the other, sometimes both at the same time, feelings like knives, that's all they know how to do. We are the rainbow necklace adorning the neck of a woman who has been too long alone confronting a monochrome world, we are the little breeze that gingerly lifts the lid of sorrow. We are the shoots that appear the day after, that cause malicious tongues to lie, the shoots that blossom against all expectation."

Thank you to Yann, always.
Twenty years is really something.